I0682750

Terraspantion Chronicles, Book 2

Time Hole

By Mit Sandru

Artwork by Dumitru Sandru

Chivileri Publishing

Copyright © 2015 by Dumitru Sandru

ISBN 13: 978-1-942612-09-4

Disclaimer:

This is a fictional story. All names, persons, organizations, businesses, occurrences, and places, except for historical locations, are fictitious and arise solely from the imagination of the author. Any resemblances to actual people or events are completely coincidental.

Table of Contents

Terraspantion Chronicles are a collection of stories narrating mankind's exploration and expansion into space by establishing bases on the Moon, Mars, asteroids, and other planets, and the adventures of those endeavors. All novels are stand-alone and can be read in any order, unless otherwise noted.

Chapter 1.

The Moon is not made of cheese. Considering the exotic minerals the Moon contains, it might as well be a blueberry muffin or a chocolate chip cookie, with the blueberries or the chocolate chips as those minerals. The ores are not native to the Moon; rather, meteors laden with minerals of all kinds crashed into it and stayed there to be discovered—or, better said—to be mined by humanity.

Unlike the Earth, where most meteors under a certain size burn up in the atmosphere, the Moon is a welcoming punching bag. Over billions of years, millions of mineral-rich meteors have smashed into the Moon and remained there, undisturbed, slightly banged up, buried just feet below the surface—or deeper, if they've been there longer—covered by the dust produced by the later impacts of their brethren. But most of the meteors land on the far side, the side unprotected by Mother Earth. That's why the Moon is hideously puckered with craters on the side we don't see, the far side.

In the 21st century, mankind took another giant leap and began mining those rare minerals: europium, terbium, yttrium, dysprosium, neodymium, and other "-ium" elements. Mankind has never been known to leave a treasure trove unclaimed. Mining entrepreneurs and international joint ventures arrived on the Moon to retrieve those riches. The technology of rockets and space equipment had advanced to the point where it was cost-effective to extract, refine, and export the minerals back to Earth.

Surviving on the Moon and undertaking the tasks required to extract the ores does not come cheap. But it is cheaper than finding and mining them on Earth, where millions of cubic meters of soil would need to be excavated and then processed to obtain a few pounds of pure rare minerals. And then there are the politics, the environmentalists, the very corrupt or slightly corrupt politicians and bureaucrats, taxes, lawyers, and many other factors that quadruple the cost of mining on Earth.

Sure, there was some political outcry from the pristine-at-heart back on Earth when mining on the Moon began, but there is no life on the Moon, unless it is taken there by expensive technology. There were no demonstrators dressed in space suits, picketing the gates of the lunar mines, marching with signs and placards demanding to "Stop Raping the Moon."

Despite its harsh environment and lack of atmosphere, the Moon is a good place for mining, and it quickly became the new Wild West. The mining entities were private consortiums, and profit dictated the nature of the operations there. Governments, at least in agreements on paper, were not interested in private endeavors. The politicians were more interested in scientific or military applications and, since the consortiums were owned by international entities, there was not much friction among governments about the mining rights, the minerals, and the profits.

The consortium International Universal Mining Inc.—abbreviated as IUM Inc., to match the name-endings of the exotic minerals—had a large mining operation in the crater Racah, at $14°$ S and $180°$ W, employing around 300 people and many more pieces of machinery that worked around the clock extracting the minerals. The crater Racah was about 60 kilometers (37 miles) in diameter, and it was full of smaller meteor craters within and outside its basin. The entire operation was set up as a hub consisting of a main station named "Racah Home Base"—affectionately known as RABi for short—where the ores were brought from the various mining stations to be refined and smelted. The processing and purification of ores had to take place on the Moon before the minerals could be sent back to Earth. That was not necessarily because of pollution, but because mass and weight costs lots of money to transport by rocket ships from the Moon.

The safest place to be on the Moon is underground. Down there, there is no danger of meteor impacts or radiation from the Sun, as there is on the lunar surface. The insulation provided by the soil against the wild variances in temperature is an added benefit. Building quarters underground was less expensive than building them aboveground, especially for an industrial and mining station like RABi.

Chapter 2.

"Dolores Da Villa, please report to the dispatch."

She was on her way to the elevator to start her six-hour shift at a lower level when she heard her name called in her ear bud, making her wonder what the nature of the emergency was. She changed direction toward the dispatch room, taking the corridor lined with pictures of pine trees. Because of the dull environment in a mining station, most interior walls were covered with panels depicting vividly colored scenes from Earth—except for desert scenes, because the whole Moon was a desert. Besides the pictures of Earth, potted green plants growing under artificial light abounded along the walls and in corners. It made the workers almost feel at home, as an advertising brochure claimed.

Dolores Da Villa was a lunar generalist and went by the nickname Deedee. A generalist had to have at least a degree in engineering: mechanical, electrical, electronics, mining, or sciences. Deedee had a master's degree, or S.M., in engineering from MIT, and she was 10 months into her third one-year contract in this financially promising mining hellhole. After each year, there was a six-month reprieve back on Earth. Deedee was an American, with a Haitian-Dominican mother and a father of Latino descent. She was a brown-skinned beauty with rare blue eyes, and she stood only five feet tall.

The vaulted ceilings underground—where there were no piping, HVAC ducting, or electrical conduits hanging from them—were painted cerulean blue, in an attempt to simulate the sky. But unlike the sky on Earth, the ceilings had lots of fingerprints and palm prints on them from people who, at one time or another, had bounced too high as they walked down the corridor, trying to keep their heads—with or without hard hats—from bumping into the ceiling.

The dispatch room was near the center of the underground compound of tunnels on the first level, at 10 meters (33 feet) beneath the surface. The offices of this base were located in a tunnel, like everything else, behind a long clear plastic wall that contained the main computers and security monitoring. The dispatch, as well as the offices for the managers, security officers, clerical workers, and communication specialists—one of each per shift—occupied these quarters as well. The office staff was maintained to the minimum necessary, and at times only a communication specialist may be in the offices area. Aside from being in a tunnel, which was the norm for living underground, the offices were very much like their counterparts on Earth, including gray padded-canvas partitions, aluminum desks and chairs, and flat monitors, some hanging from the ceiling.

"Hey, Samir," Deedee addressed the current and only dispatcher on duty.

"Deedee! I have the perfect job for you," said the Indian man, eyeing her passively.

"I thought I was assigned to check on the rock grinder on third below," she replied.

"Well, the grinder can wait. We have an emergency at K204." Samir was referring to the satellite crater about 80 kilometers, as a lunar crow flies, outside Racah's rim. "The second compressor has failed in as many weeks. They are down to one, and, if the last one fails, we'll have to carry out an emergency flight delivery. You know what that means." Samir whistled and spiraled one finger up in the air, indicating the high cost of a rocket flight from RABi to the K204 satellite mining station.

On the Moon, there were only two methods of travel: driving or flying. And a flight, in the absence of air, was only by rocket engine, which was 1,000% more expensive than land travel.

"You're out of your mind, Samir." Deedee placed her hands on her hips. "We're in the middle of the lunar night on the surface. It's dangerous to drive in the dark."

Roads connected RABi to all the other satellite mines; actually, they weren't roads but dirt paths made by lunar bulldozers that leveled the meteorite potholes and pushed small rocks aside to permit a somewhat straighter and less bumpy ride. Land transportation usually happened during sunlight, preferably after sunrise or before sunset, when the Sun was lower on the horizon, to reduce radiation exposure. A full cycle of day and night on the Moon was equal to about 27.5 Earth days, or almost 14 Earth days for each day and night.

"Come on, it's not that dangerous." Samir tried to play down the risk by giving her a fake placating smile.

"Really! Like one in 20 transports over eight hours at night ends up in a crater," Deedee retorted heatedly. "That's over 225 kilometers of twisted road driving. At night." She raised her hand to make her point.

The added danger to the night driving was the lack of light. The vehicles had headlights, but they consumed electricity and their batteries wouldn't last long. Instead, for visibility, the drivers used night vision goggles.

"By road it's 281 kilometers, but it's an emergency. We have to do this before the production at K204, or more precisely, at mining substation S18 stops." Samir raised his hands and eyebrows in concern. The quotas had to be reached, and no one took that lightly.

Deedee shook her head in frustration. "Let me understand this: It will take two people over 24 hours to go by surface, but it will take less than 10 minutes to fly, with less risk. What kind of logic is that?" She thumped her forehead with the heel of her palm.

"It's a lot less expensive by road," said Samir, now showing no concern. "You can have the best lunar specialist driver. Your choice." Samir wobbled his head side to side in the customary affirmative gesture of his Mumbai hometown.

Specialists were the cadres who performed the same jobs every day, the sometimes-boring grunt work on the Moon. Higher education was not required, but technical expertise was a prerequisite. The Moon was a tough place to inhabit and—in case of accidents—to survive in. Technical expertise was the difference between death and surviving long enough to be rescued.

"Why did you pick me? This should be handled by a specialist, an LVD." She was talking about a Lunar Vehicle Driver.

"Oh yes—I almost forgot." Samir grinned. "The failed compressors and their controllers need to be evaluated as to why they failed. You were not selected only for your driving skills but your technical skills as well."

Phony flattery did not impress Deedee. She made a gesture as if to refuse the task, but then, considering the double pay for hazardous duty on the surface, she changed her mind. "I want a generalist as my co-driver," she demanded.

"Huh? OK. Let me see." Samir consulted his computer. "You've got three to choose from, and they are in the break room right now. Which one?" Samir motioned to one of the screens near the ceiling showing the break room and its occupants.

Rather than pick one of them from the screen, Deedee left the dispatch and went to the break room, not far down the corridor. The so-called break room was the mess hall, the coffee room, the general rec room, and everything in between, located at the intersection of two corridors. As Deedee approached the entrance, the smell of fresh-brewed coffee and donuts wafted her way. Three generalists, identified by red jumpsuits just like hers, were drinking coffee and BS-ing before their shift started. She knew all three men, but something told her to select the biggest of them.

"Arno, are you left-handed?"

"Sure am, Deedee." He raised his left hand, holding up his aluminum coffee cup.

"Good. I have a job for you. C'mon." She motioned for him to follow her.

"Uh-oh, Deedee's going to give Arno a job," said one of the generalists, while the other one burst out laughing.

Deedee flashed them both of her middle fingers, one for each, of course, which caused more snickering. A woman had to be tough in this male-dominated environment.

"What do you expect from two Californians? From the land of fruits and nuts." She left quickly before giving them the chance to respond—or the satisfaction.

Arnold Bacher, nicknamed Arno, was a generalist who was four months into his first one-year contract. He was junior to Deedee in terms of his experience on the Moon, although he had a PhD in science from Caltech. Though an American of Italian and German descent, he looked Scandinavian, judging by his blond hair, light-blue eyes, and six-foot frame. Because of his height, he barely qualified for a lunar generalist job; shorter, smaller people were preferred. Mass costs money to transport.

As they were about to enter the dispatch, Arno caught up with Deedee. "What's this job all about?"

"Critical mission," she said as she opened the door and stepped inside. "At least that's what dispatcher Samir wants us to believe." She stared with one eyebrow raised at Samir.

Samir assessed Arno up and down. "Him? Why him?"

"Because he's big," said Deedee. "And he's left-handed."

Arno narrowed his eyes at Deedee.

"Whatever." Samir busied himself on the keyboard, entering the details of the mission to K204.

"Are we going somewhere?" asked Arno.

"Yes, to K204," replied Deedee.

"Are we going to fly?"

"We're driving."

"Isn't that dangerous? And what's all that about being big and left-handed?" Arno furrowed his eyebrows.

"In case of an accident, you look powerful enough to rescue me."

"I'm a generalist, for crying out loud, not a truck driver." Arno folded his arms and stared at the rocky ceiling adorned with air ducts, pipes, and electrical wire raceways.

"You are a jack-of-all-trades, just like me," said Deedee. "We have to take care of the job at hand. If you don't like it, you can quit."

"Quit, huh? Did you read the fine print in your contract? If you quit or get fired, the company will deduct the cost of lunar living from your pay until the next transport is available to bring you home." Arno gave a short nod to make his point.

"So?"

"You even have to pay for the air you breathe in here. You have to keep your job in this zoo."

"Well, Arno, Luna is not as forgiving and hospitable as Mother Earth is. You knew the job was tough when you took it."

Arno mumbled something under his breath and waved his hand in dismissal. He leaned over Samir's shoulder to read the manifest. "We're transporting compressors to K204, mining substation S18?"

"Yes," said Samir, unperturbed. "And you'll take with you, among other things, water, nitrogen tetroxide, and hydrazine. These last two will be on a trailer hitched to your truck." Samir stopped and looked at the gloomy team. "Well, I sent the manifest to your PCs."

A PC was a personal computer, and everyone on the Moon had one. But it was not the PC of long ago;

instead, it was an oversized watch worn around the wrist that served not only as a source of information but as a communicator as well, and it was connected to the ear bud on every worker. Having voice command capability, a PC was mandatory for any lunar worker to provide or obtain instructions and emergency response information. It was a computer, tablet, smart phone with camera, and audio-video entertainment unit.

"Your ETD is in one hour from garage #4." Samir smirked at Arno. "Your 'estimated time to departure' for the newbies." He turned back to his screen. "Go. Do what you need to do before your ELA, external lunar activity."

Arno turned pink, having had enough of this verbal abuse. "If this ends badly, I'll kill you. Both of you," he said, pointing a finger from one to the other.

"Not unless I kill him first," said Deedee, glaring at Samir.

Chapter 3.

After gathering and placing their belongings for the trip in a cylindrical pressurized case, Arno and Deedee proceeded to Suit Room G, or SR-G for short. Every lunar worker had a space suit assigned to him or her, and the suits were kept in SRs designated by functions. "G" stood for generalists. Each outfit consisted of two suits: the outer space suit made for the harsh, external environment and the inner suit that molded to a person's body, was pressurized, and contained the heating, cooling, moisture discharge, and other personal hygiene removal systems. The outer space suits were standard issue, in four convenient sizes; there were no tailor-made space suits for anyone here, unless you were a visiting executive or VIP or the director of the mining station, who was currently absent.

The inner suit was a unitard with attached socks, hood, and gloves. It also functioned as the last line of defense against any breach of the outer suit, and it was the only component custom-made for each user. The hood, which covered a person's hair to keep it in place, contained headphones and audiovisual gear; small microphones, one on either side of the mouth, were also embedded in the hood. The audiovisual gear resembled a large pair of goggles, which acted as transitional sun lenses when needed, and they had displays for the PC and the suit's computer, including mini-screens for the forward and rear cameras that were mounted on the outer suit. The interior upper rim of the goggles held the LED strip panel displaying the oxygen level, temperature, humidity, and electrical power status, among other necessary information.

Deedee and Arno entered two small private rooms and dressed in their personal inner suits first, after removing their regular indoor jumpsuits. Each suit fit them like a glove and had to be worn on bare skin, commando-style. They kept their PCs on their wrists, maintaining skin contact for the bio-monitoring capability. Outside in the locker room, as they were retrieving their bulkier outer suits, Arno didn't fail to notice Deedee's proportional body—firm breasts and buttocks, not too big but not too small. The pleasure of watching her body in the tight suit, sans panty line, was interrupted by her glare, as if to remind him of the sexual harassment courses he had received as part of his employment education. Slightly embarrassed, he made himself busy with his outer suit, avoiding her stare.

Although the outer suits came in four standard sizes to fit different heights, they were adjustable to accommodate the length of each user's limbs and torso. Besides maintaining a low pressure atmosphere, the space suit's purpose was to shelter and protect the lunar walker from the Moon's harsh environment: from scrapes and bruises, the vacuum, the radiation, and the temperature variations. In other words, it was a body capsule, allowing the lunar walker to perform nearly all the movements a person could perform on Earth, except for the ability to scratch certain parts of his or her body if he or she had an itch. On the positive side, it had its own porta-potty.

The outer space suit was composed of a body suit, gloves, boots, and a shoulder unit. Deedee and Arno entered their suits through the shoulders' oval openings, which were large enough so that no external help was needed to suit up. Once they were in the suits, they placed the shoulder units, which contained the suit's computer, external lights, and cameras—not to mention the many ports for life support, power, and communication. The shoulder units contained the helmets, but unlike the helmets of yesteryear that were bulky, hard, and prone to cracking if hit with a sharp object, these helmets were pliable and made of transparent plastic, resembling a half dome when pressurized. Because they were made of soft material, the helmets could be opened from the front and folded back like a hood when not needed.

After the shoulder units self-sealed to the outer suit and to the inner suit around the neck, Deedee and Arno put on their Suit Life Support units, or SLSs, which resembled a life vest with front and back units. They connected the SLSs to the ports on their shoulder units. Additional batteries were mounted on pockets on the suits' outer thighs and calves; this arrangement was to ensure an even distribution of weight and to lower their centers of gravity.

Their PCs connected and synchronized with the suits' computers. They placed their soft helmets over their heads, sealed them, and then pressurized the suits by voice command. Each helmet became a half-dome bubble with 360-degree visibility. The final act was to put their space gloves on and seal them to the suit. The inner suit was pressurized to the Earth's atmospheric pressure. The outer suit was pressurized to only 1% of Earth air pressure. While still indoors, the outer suit wrinkled snugly against their bodies. This dual-suit pressurization provided for easiest movements while in the vacuum. If the outer suit was at full atmospheric pressure, it would inflate like a balloon, and walking would be difficult.

Even though they were in an atmospherically breathable environment in the suit room, after pressurization they would rely on the SLSs for their air and all their environmental needs from that point on. The entire suit weighed 50 kilograms on Earth, but on the Moon it weighed only nine kilos. Satisfied that their suits operated within their parameters, Deedee and Arno walked to garage #4.

In the depressurized garage, the transport vehicle was ready for the mission. The Moon vacuum was awaiting them. They entered the airlock chamber, closed the hatch behind them, and pressed a big red button to depressurize. The needle of the pressure gauge on the wall as well as the digital gauge started dropping—when it comes to a vacuum, it pays to have different redundant sensors to tell you if you'll live or die. The pressure dropped as far as the vacuum pumps could extract, almost to a near vacuum, and a valve opened, letting the last molecules of air escape outside. Their outer suits bulked up slightly as the low pressure inside them overcame the vacuum. Deedee and Arno checked the indicators of their space suits to ensure that all systems were working properly.

The vacuum was an unforgiving environment. If they were without their suits, especially the inner suits, and were exposed to an instant vacuum, the gas in their bodies would inflate their muscles, lungs, and stomach, killing them in a short time. And if they didn't die from the gas expansion in their lungs and stomach, they would die from their blood boiling—actually gasifying—and the rest of their bodies possibly ripping apart. Of course, over a period of time, their bodies would freeze-dry from the extremely low temperatures and become mummies. Whatever would be left of a space walker would not be a pretty sight.

Chapter 4.

On the panel, a red light with a black skull and crossbones turned on, indicating a fully depressurized chamber. Arno opened the oval latch and swung it up to the ceiling. He and Deedee stepped outside into the vacuum of garage #4.

"Everything is a go, from what I see on my monitor." They heard the disembodied voice of Samir, who doubled as the ELA, the external lunar activity, supervisor. "I'll open the garage's exterior gate when you are ready to roll."

"Roger. Wilco," replied Deedee, acknowledging receipt of the audio and their compliance with the mission at hand.

The transport lunar vehicle resembled a flatbed truck with four large metallic-mesh wheels and a cabin of roundish geometry, resembling a skull or a jack-o-lantern, depending on whether you were afraid or excited to experience the Moon's surface in a total vacuum. It had a cattle guard, not so much to protect from any lunar bovines but to push aside any rocks over a certain size from its path. The guard resembled teeth, which complemented the cabin's skull-like appearance. Several pressurized cylinders with supplies were packed on the flatbed, along with the two compressors, a few more boxy containers, and another large cylindrical tank containing water. Considering the balmy temperature of -50°C in the garage, the water in the cylindrical tank was about to become solid ice, unless it was already frozen. There was no fear of the tank rupturing as the water froze because the tank contained a gas bladder, which shrank as the ice expanded. A two-wheel trailer containing two spherical tanks with the rocket fuel was hitched to the truck. The yellow lettering indicated which tank contained what chemical. The lunar truck's four large mesh wheels, each over a meter in diameter, flanked the flatbed. Each wheel had its own independent electric motor and was capable of turning in tandem as well. Dust guards covered the top of the wheels.

"Everything seems to be tied down and ready to go." Arno walked around the truck, inspecting it but without kicking the nonexistent tires, and then disconnected its electrical power supply line.

"You'll ride shotgun, Arno." Deedee climbed onto the flatbed and opened the round hatch on the back of the cabin. She climbed into the depressurized cabin, feet first, while holding onto the interior handles.

Arno followed, and soon after they settled in, they took inventory of the instrument panel indicators, making sure everything signaled a "go." Their PCs linked to the truck's computer as well.

"Commence pressurizing the cabin," announced Arno.

"Roger, pressurization," acknowledged Samir, the ELA supervisor.

While keeping an eye on the pressurization indicator, Arno and Deedee connected the truck's power and environmental life support tubes to their shoulder ports and then removed their SLS units, storing them behind the seats. The cabin pressure light turned green.

"Cabin is pressurized," said Arno.

"All systems go," pronounced Deedee.

"Roger that," came the answer from the ELA supervisor.

"Equalize cabin pressure with our suits," said Deedee.

"Roger," said the ELA supervisor.

Deedee and Arno unsealed the front of their helmets and folded them back like a hood. Next, they removed their outer space-suit gloves for better tactile ability. For safety reasons, they would keep their space suits on.

"We're ready to roll," announced Deedee.

"Roger that," acknowledged the ELA supervisor. "The garage gate will open in five seconds."

The "garage gate" was a longitudinally rectangular, convex hatch with rounded corners. It opened upward, swinging toward the ceiling like an old-fashioned tilt-up garage door. Once it cleared the threshold, two ramps rose and were placed automatically over the threshold so that the truck's wheels would not damage the seals at the bottom.

"OK, Arno, take it away," Deedee said.

Arno reached over to the knobby joystick on the middle console, pressed the center button, and pulled the joystick back, nudging the truck over the threshold ramps and onto the lunar soil in the exit tunnel. They drove to the surface through a semicircular corrugated metal tunnel, and soon they were outside, under the stars of the Milky Way.

"Normal egress," Arno intoned.

"Systems operating at normal," confirmed Deedee, while a few beeps sounded and digital numbers flickered on the panels, keeping track of the mission's parameters.

"Roger that," said the ELA supervisor. "Good luck and keep in touch."

"We will, except when we have satellite blackouts. Deedee out."

Arno pulled the joystick back to a dizzying speed of 15 km per hour. As needed he would use the same joystick to steer. "Now I get it." Arno looked at Deedee. "You wanted a lefty so you can ride in the driver's seat, which makes sense with a joystick on the center console."

"Arno, you're a genius."

"Do you always need to be in control?"

"Only when I supervise big white males," Deedee smirked.

"I promise I'll be gentle." Arno kept his eyes on the road, moving the joystick to follow the bends in the road.

Deedee looked at him, amused, then turned her head to observe the landscape. The terrain outside their home station was as dull as the sand in a desert, but gray in color. Sure, they were close to one of the Racah's rims, which gave the impression of a range of hills on the nearby horizon but, besides that, there was just moon dust puckered by meteor craters and mining holes. Even the station's nearby surface compounds—painted in vivid colors and resembling abandoned, California-desert shacks with rocky flat roofs—were more interesting than the landscape. The surface observation deck, which allowed workers to admire the lunar surface from the comfort of a breathable atmosphere, was a half-round clear plastic tube resembling a greenhouse. This 30-meter-long promenade was covered by a flat roof with soil and rocks on it for protection against meteorites and harmful radiation from the Sun.

On the surface, farther away, there were half-round greenhouses, now dark, which supplied the base with green-leaf vegetables and legumes when the Sun shined. The lunar day lasted only two weeks, but the sunshine was around the clock during that time, and the plants grew fast. There were solar panel fields, but they were there more for advertising clean energy than to supply ample amounts of electricity. The bulk of the electrical power needed for this industrial site came from a nuclear reactor.

Along the road were the innumerable boot marks of previous astronauts who had either worked outside or enjoyed ELAs. The boot marks were there forever, unless someone else stepped on them. Some jokers from past Halloweens even created graves, scribbling RIP in the dust. And, of course, the mandatory heart shapes with the names of lovers, couples, or by-now-divorced pairs were abundant. Even here humans left trash behind, a bottle here and there, a tin can, some piece of discarded machinery, and even an occasional odd object like a yellow rubber boot.

Nearby, two hangars with flat retractable roofs contained two lunar flying crafts, tail numbers CRAB-A and CRAB-B, to be used only when absolutely necessary, according to Samir. The lunar crafts, which were capable of achieving orbit, were nicknamed "the flying potatoes" because of their cabin shapes. Farther away, the landing field was empty; no rocket from Earth was parked there now.

The transmission tower's red light blinked periodically. That was to be the last sign of civilization Deedee and Arno would see until they'd reach their destination.

Chapter 5.

"So, Deedee, are you married? Or have a boyfriend, perhaps?" Arno broke the silence.

"No, I'm unattached. How about you, Arno?"

"Just like you, unattached."

"How come no woman has claimed you? You're such a catch."

"Well, not that I've sworn celibacy or anything, and I have sampled and will continue to sample the delights of female companionship, but I felt that once I was tied down, I couldn't take risks in space or the Moon— or soon, Mars. I'd like very much to go to Mars."

"Over half the men and women here on the Moon are married. They even have children back home. It doesn't seem to bother them."

"Everyone to his or her own life and comfort level. Once I get tied down, I'd like to spend my time with my mate. And my kids." He smiled.

"With that kind of mentality, you would be a great catch."

"I would? Don't tell me you have a sister you want to set me up with."

"Ha, ha, ha. That was just a compliment," said Deedee.

"So what about you, why aren't you tied down?"

"Oh, many reasons. Maybe I haven't met the right one yet."

"Right, the crowd here on the Moon does not offer an abundant selection. The men here are either married, gamblers, or major risk takers."

"Who said anything about a man?"

"Pardon me. My mistake." He turned red.

"Gotcha!" Deedee snickered. "I like men."

"You're toying with me."

"Maybe. Besides, since you're not married, you must be one of those gamblers or risk takers."

He looked at her and smiled. "You have beautiful blue eyes."

She glanced sideways at him and shook her head, amused. She did have beautiful blue eyes and, in combination with her light-brown complexion, she was yummy attractive. She knew that. The trip had just started and he was hitting on her already, although she didn't mind his comment. But it would be better not to continue with this subject; they had a job to do.

"You wanna talk about science?" he asked, observing her reaction.

"No."

"Philosophy?"

"No."

"Women's needs?"

"Just drive. We have a long way to go, and we don't have to exhaust all the subjects at once."

Arno speeded up to 25 km/h. "OK. I'll amuse myself with the joystick," he said, sulking.

Each large wheel had an independent electric motor drive with synchronized speeds to adjust for when the truck turned. The spokes on the wheels were curved for additional cushioning when riding on the dirt roads. The wheels' wire mesh—pneumatic tires were out of the question—were intended to provide enough grip and not accumulate soil. The 25 km/h speed would seem like a crawl on Earth but not on the Moon, where the horizon was just a rock's throw away, like the edge of an upcoming chasm. The dirt road was another reason to drive slowly: A vehicle bounces a lot higher on the Moon. But even if there were paved roads, safe speeds would still be low, because low weight meant low friction, and any vehicle going over 50 km/h would skid off the road when braking or on curves, and end up in a meteor crater, usually upside down.

Chapter 6.

"Time to turn the headlights off and switch to night vision," announced Deedee after a minute.

Lights consumed electricity and would drain the batteries too fast. Driving in the dark aided by night vision goggles was safe, in theory. Although the dark side of the Moon did not benefit from the Sun's reflected light from Earth, in the absence of atmosphere and clouds, the Milky Way provided plenty of light. The terrain ahead of them, seen through their night vision goggles, was a greenish, shadowless landscape. It was the lack of shadows that caused hazards when driving at night—a boulder or a hole was difficult to distinguish on the road. Sometimes even the road was hard to discern, although it had red-white striped markers spaced every 100 meters to delineate it.

"RABi, this is surface mission to K204. We went to night vision," reported Deedee.

"This is Martha at RABi, your night communication connection. Roger that, night vision. How are you doing out there, kids?" Martha was a grandmother but only in her forties. She was the only grandmother on the Moon as far as anyone knew, and she was a hot mama, as far as many lunar men opined.

"Peachy, Martha," said Deedee. "Could you play better music on your radio station?"

"Anything you want, as long as it's talk."

"We'll contact you in an hour." Deedee concluded the transmission to the home base. "This is boring," she sighed.

"What would you like to talk about?" asked Arno.

"Nothing. Do you have something in mind?"

"Nothing," said Arno just as unenthusiastically, but then he remembered something that was bothering him. "Why did Samir assign you this mission?"

"Officially or unofficially?"

Arno looked at her for a moment and said, "Unofficially."

"I think the son of a bitch is trying to get back at me."

"Why? What did you do?"

"It's what I didn't do. I didn't respond to his advances, even when I reminded him that he's married with a bunch of kids back home."

"Samir? That little brown rat," said Arno. "Sorry."

"Don't worry. I can take care of myself."

"Can I ask why you selected me?"

"I really don't know. Somehow, out of the three of you there in the coffee room, you caught my attention. I hope you don't mind."

"Well, maybe I do, but here I am now, and we'll let it ride."

"Good," said Deedee. "I'm going to play some jazz in my headphones."

"If we ignore the union rules and alternate driving, we could get there sooner, without having to stop and rest after ten hours," Arno proposed.

"Yeah, let's do that. You drive for four hours, then I'll drive for four while you sleep."

Arno was driving on his second four-hour leg, after Deedee had completed hers, when he observed something strange ahead—a completely flat surface, like a frozen lake. He blinked to make sure he was not seeing a mirage, but the surface grew larger as they approached it.

"Deedee, wake up!" he shouted.

"Wh-what?" she mumbled, awakening from her sleep.

"Do you have your night vision on?"

"No, but even without it, I can see a light patch ahead of us. You'd better stop."

Arno did not hesitate in bringing the lunar truck to a halt.

Deedee turned on her night vision and stared. "What is that? It looks like a salt flat in the desert. Or maybe ice? No, it couldn't be ice."

"Ice?" he snickered at the notion. There was no such thing as surface ice on the Moon. "That's not a salt flat, either. It's a wall or crevice of some kind."

"Let's drive closer to it, and then we'll turn the lights on."

"Roger that." Arno pulled back the joystick, and the truck advanced at quarter-speed toward whatever lay across the road.

Both of them were mesmerized and intrigued by what that apparition could be.

"Arno, stop!" Deedee shouted.

"We're 30 meters from it," replied Arno.

"Look at our instruments."

"There seems to be a slight interference, but nothing worrisome."

"Turn the lights on!" Deedee said loudly.

Chapter 7.

Arno gave a voice command and the two headlights on top of the cabin flooded the road and the landscape ahead of them.

"It's a frickin' crater," she said.

"What the hell is it doing in the middle of the road?" Arno wondered.

"Are we still on the road?" She looked outside and then at the rearview monitor. "Yes, we are. Get a few meters closer. Slowly."

Arno inched the joystick forward, getting nearer to the large hole ahead of them. "This doesn't look right." He stopped the truck.

"A meteor must have crashed smack into the middle of our road," Deedee commented. "I didn't hear anything about this."

"You're right," he said. "Considering the size of the crater . . ." He punched orders into the onboard distance finder. "It's 294.4 meters across. That's as wide as three football fields. This meteor had to have been a big boy."

"This close to our base, we should have detected seismic quakes." She leaned forward, mystified.

"Maybe it crashed after we left," he speculated. Without Deedee giving the order, he moved the truck a few yards closer to the rim.

"Stop, Arno. It's dangerous."

"What do you mean?"

"Look at it." Deedee waved her hand at the crater. "It's as if this hole were scooped out of the ground."

He looked back and forth from Deedee to the crater, trying to understand what she said. "Yeah, you're right—clean-cut edges and no ejected matter forming a berm around the rim."

"We should have seen a small hill ahead of us, not a hole," she concluded.

"Now what, Captain?" Arno asked.

Deedee narrowed her eyes and stared outside. "It looks to me that we can turn back, go around it, or inspect this hole first. We must contact RABi."

"We're in a blackout," said Arno. "Estimated time until the next satellite is two minutes."

"Crap." She bit her lower lip. "Look at the walls. They look smooth."

"Should we get closer?"

"No. We could slide in. This may be a cave-in. Let's wait for the satellite."

The time passed slower than usual, it seemed, but soon enough the transmitter indicator turned green.

Deedee did not waste a second. "RABi, this is surface mission to K204, do you copy?"

"Roger, K204 mission. Martha speaking."

"We have an obstacle in the road."

"Repeat, please."

"We just passed marker 131.2, and there is a 294-meters-wide crater across the road."

"Roger that. Can you go around it?" Martha asked.

"We could, or we could turn back." Deedee looked with concern at Arno. "This is not a regular crater."

"K204 mission, let me patch you in to the base manager on duty. Actually, the only manager we have around here now."

Deedee and Arno waited for another minute, staring at the strange depression ahead of them.

"This is RABi. Manager Lai speaking."

"Roger, RABi. We need directions on how to proceed," asked Deedee.

"How big is the crater? Can you navigate around it?"

"It's huge—294 meters across," replied Deedee. "We could go around it, I guess."

"Are you willing and equipped to explore the crater before deciding to go around it or return?" Manager Lai asked.

Deedee and Arno exchanged quizzical looks.

Arno nodded. "Finally! Something worth doing."

"Yes, we are," said Deedee. "We can conduct a preliminary inspection of the rim and the immediate surroundings to determine if we can drive around it."

"Very well. Exploration authorized. I'll leave it up to you whether one or both of you exit the vehicle. And remember, safety first."

"Roger that. We'll communicate the results shortly." Deedee concluded the transmission. "Well?" She looked questioningly at Arno.

"I'd like to go. I'm curious," he said, looking at the crater with keen interest.

"OK, Arno. You exit, and I'll stay in the cab. Prepare for depressurization."

"But Captain what's-his-name always beamed down first to inspect the situation," he challenged her in jest, while pulling his hood over his head.

"That's right, and if you survive this, you'll know better when you're a captain." Deedee gave Arno a captain-knows-best look. "The captain always stays with the ship." She pointed to the vehicle. "The expendables are sent out to explore and report back. If they make it back."

Arno shook his head inside his soft helmet. Deedee pulled her helmet over her head and, after their helmets were sealed, they mounted their SLSs and disconnected the environmental truck supply from their suits. She punched the depressurize button and waited.

"Be careful, Arno. It's only -200°C outside."

"Colder than Antarctica, but, on the plus side, there is no wind," Arno quipped.

"This must be your lucky day," said Deedee.

Crossing his eyes, Arno gave her a goofy grin.

Chapter 8.

The cabin pressure's idiot light, with its customary skull and crossbones, turned red. Deedee opened the equalizer valve, and the inside of their cabin became as airless as the outside. Arno slid the back hatch open, got hold of the ceiling handles, and extricated himself from the cabin. He climbed down the ladder—each rung could accommodate only one lunar boot at a time—and landed safely on the powdery but well-packed Moon soil.

"One giant step for an educated man, one small step for a lunar truck driver like me," he proclaimed.

"Good. Keep it that way," said Deedee from inside. "Hey, tether yourself to the truck. I don't feel like getting out of my cozy cabin to save your behind."

"Aye, aye, Captain." Arno strapped a utility rope on a ring on his suit, attached it to a hook on the truck, and walked calmly to the crater's edge 20 meters away. The rope followed his trail as he uncoiled it. At the edge, he stopped and admired the view, as if he were a tourist admiring a big hole in the ground, like the Grand Canyon. He even lifted a hand above his helmet as if shielding his eyes from an unseen sun.

"Report, Arno," Deedee demanded.

"It's a big hole, and guess what? It's not a crater."

"Repeat that: What's not a crater?"

"The crater looks like a bowl—a giant glass bowl."

"Arno, check your CO_2. Are you going trippy on me?"

He turned from the edge and looked back at the truck, while pointing to the crater behind him. "I'm serious. It looks like a giant glass bowl, blue-green and smooth but dull at the same time. Almost velvety. I've never seen anything like this. Let me send you images." Arno turned to face the bowl and activated his front camera.

Deedee looked in dismay at the perfectly round, smooth but dull, blue-green bowl. No such thing could exist in nature unless it was made by . . . Who could make such a thing? The Chinese? No, this was not man-made.

"I'll relay this information to RABi. Let them go ballistic on what we discovered." She contacted home base without delay. "RABi, this is surface mission to K204, do you copy?"

"Roger, K204 mission. What's the good news?" Martha asked.

"The crater resembles a giant, blue-green bowl, round and smooth on the inside."

"Repeat pl—" The communication with RABi ended abruptly. The image Arno sent on the monitor flickered and died.

Deedee saw Arno creeping closer to the edge. "Arno, don't get any closer. That thing is interfering with our transmission."

Arno turned to look back at her, but as he turned, one boot lost its grip on the smooth dust and he slid toward the edge. He wobbled. Instead of falling face down away from the edge, he reached for the rope to stabilize himself, but the rope was slack, with a few unfurled coils on the ground, and he couldn't pull enough of it fast enough to regain his upright position. He tilted backward and fell over the edge.

Chapter 9.

The rope finally went taut, but, a second later, it snapped and jerked back from the edge toward the truck.

Deedee saw all this as if it were happening in slow motion and froze with fear. "Jeeesus! Arno, come in! Are you OK? Arno, do you copy?"

He did not respond. She crawled out of the cabin and jumped out without using the ladder—a dangerous maneuver, as she could have torn open her space suit. But she was lucky, and she landed on her feet without getting snagged on any sharp protrusions. Without thinking, she ran to the edge, but the immensity of the bowl ahead of her scared her and stopped her from getting any closer. The rope Arno had used resembled a snake on the ground. She picked it up and tied it to one of the rings on her suit. Cautiously, walking with one foot ahead while leaning back, she approached the edge.

It was a giant glass bowl, or at least that's what it looked like. Maybe it was a radio dish antenna? In the center of the bowl there was a bright hole, but where was Arno? There! She spotted him as he came to a stop at the bottom near the bright hole. She gasped with terror. Using the magnification on her goggles, she saw the awful situation Arno was in. He was sitting at the edge of the hole, apparently with his feet dangling over. He was looking down into the hole as if contemplating jumping in.

"Arno, come in! Arno, this is Deedee, come in!"

No response from him.

Deedee assessed the situation quickly. Her teammate had either suffered a concussion sliding down or had lost his marbles, contemplating his imminent death on the edge of the abyss. By all appearances there wasn't any way of getting down to the bottom. Although the bowl was 294 meters in diameter, the bottom seemed to be only about 100 meters down. Arno needed immediate rescuing.

Her mouth dried up from her panicked breathing, but, if she didn't move fast, Arno would be another fatality on the Moon. The winch at the front of the truck was the answer. She retreated slowly and then ran-hopped back to the truck, sliding to a stop in a cloud of dust, which settled quickly. She unknotted the rope, placed the hook from the winch's cable on her belt ring, and then engaged the safety latch. She gave terse verbal orders to transfer the command of the winch to her PC.

"Winch on. Pay out one meter per second." The winch turned, allowing her to walk to the edge with some degree of safety.

At the edge she stopped the winch from paying out any more cable. Arno was in the same place and position. His speedy retrieval was of the utmost importance, considering this mysterious bowl. Her safety depended on a 3-millimeter-thick stainless steel cable, an electric motor that could pull ten Arnos, and her ability to rappel down the bowl's walls without chafing or cutting the cable on the edge of the bowl, which surprisingly wasn't sharp. She was no mountain climber, but she was Arno's only hope. Holding onto the thin cable with both gloved hands, she swallowed hard and approached the edge, walking sideways.

The cable was taut, and both of her boots' heels were on the edge, her back toward the bowl. Taking a deep breath, she gave the order to the winch to pay out at 10 centimeters per second. Holding onto the cable, she leaned back, and everything was going well until she reached the 45-degree inclination. That's where the tricky part began. She had to keep leaning back, cable taut, until she reached a horizontal position and could commence walking backward down the wall while holding on to the cable.

But she didn't.

Chapter 10.

She flipped backward, head down, feet in the air, with the cable vibrating between her legs. Her helmet bounced off the wall like a balloon. Her upside-down position didn't last for long, as her butt slid down and she regained her center of gravity. The winch continued paying out the cable, and she slid slowly along the wall, held by a ring on her belt and the cable. She inspected the wall she was sliding down on, afraid that its roughness might shred her outer suit, but the wall was smooth as glass, although fuzzy at the same time.

The descent was excruciatingly slow. Would the cable hold, or would it chafe on the edge and eventually break? She decided to chance it, and she increased the speed to one meter per second. At that rate, she might reach the flatter bottom in about two minutes. Maybe.

But the flat bottom did not come. The wall curved from the vertical into a steep slope until it reached a 45-degree angle. Even at this angle, Deedee couldn't regain her upright position, and she continued sliding on her behind. A couple of minutes later, the curvature steepened again. This was not a flat-bottomed bowl; it now resembled the upper part of an hourglass. The view from the top was an optical illusion, and now she was accelerating down the funnel portion of this strange hole, or whatever it was.

For a moment she felt an unusual vertigo attack, wondering where she was. She looked up, and the sky was shrinking into a smaller circle, although the circle wobbled and then it stabilized. Yes, she was descending to get Arno. Should she stop? Abandon Arno and save herself from this hole? No, she couldn't do that. Arno was her responsibility. She looked at the thin cable. Even if it held, was there enough length to get to Arno? She decided to worry about that when it happened.

The good news was that Arno was near, and the cable was holding.

The bad news was that she wasn't getting closer fast enough, and he wasn't responding to her calls. Increasing the speed seemed unadvisable. She bit her lip, hoping for salvation—hers and his. Arno kept still, sitting motionless on some invisible ledge on the wall of this curious hourglass pit. The wall was steep but soon she got close enough to him. She slowed the winch's payout speed until she was near Arno and then stopped it. Pulling on the cable, she planted her feet on the dull wall, but surprisingly, she was standing upright on a ledge. She never noticed this ledge before, but for sure now, she felt it and saw it. Arno was sitting down at the edge of the same ledge, an arm's-length away.

"Is he even alive?" she wondered out loud. She approached him, holding onto the cable and hoping not to see his face with lifeless eyes and his tongue sticking out.

Chapter 11.

Deedee walked closer to Arno. With his hands on his lap, sitting on the ledge and leaning forward, he was stock-still. The wall—the very steep wall—seemed to be as slick as ice, she noticed, but somehow fuzzy as well, and the ledge must have been made from the same stuff. She hoped that Arno wouldn't slip off it.

She extended her arm and grabbed him by the SLS harness, giving him a shake while shouting into her mic, "Arno! Can you hear me?"

He jolted as if awakening from sleepwalk. "Deedee? What are you doing here?"

She didn't waste any time. She picked up the end of the remaining rope Arno had used as a tether and tied it to the hook on the cable. Then she plugged her comm-link into Arno's shoulder unit port. Arno's vitals appeared in her visor. Everything was normal.

"Arno, are you OK?"

"Sure am," he said without a trace of worry.

"Do you know where you are?"

He looked around. "Sure. We're in some kind of circular amphitheater."

Deedee looked around, and her jaw dropped. The smooth hourglass-like bowl had become a round amphitheater, just as Arno said. He was sitting on the ledge, which had become some kind of circular path, dangling his feet, and overlooking a swirling well of light down below. All around them were concentric pathways, from where they stood all the way to the rim. The rings did not continue down the well, as far as she could see. It seems that the paths were discernible only when looking up. Looking down the wall of the funnel was smooth as glass.

The circular paths were not concentric but helical, she observed after a closer examination. The material—if the substance making the funnel and paths could be called that—might not be solid at all, although it felt solid under her boots. There was something else—a mist, a gaseous fog, that seemed to move down the helical path. She waved her arm through it, but it posed no restriction nor did she disturb its fluffy formation. It was not gas, but something else: an indescribable flowing body of something she had never seen before.

"Arno, what is this?" She waved her hands at the surroundings.

"Hell if I know. Or maybe I do. I woke up down here after I fell in."

"Why are you looking down that hole?"

"It's mesmerizing. You see that swirling vortex, going down and down the shaft? It leads to infinity. Into another universe." He bobbed his head inside his helmet.

Infinity? Another universe?

She knew better than to look down into the hole. That thing, flowing slowly around them and creating the vortex down the well, had a hypnotic effect, and she, too, could be entranced by it. "Arno, we've got to go back."

"You're right. Is the truck up there?" He looked at the thin cable extending to the rim. "You came to rescue me. Thanks, Deedee." He stood up and brushed his suit bottom to clear some unseen sand.

"Are you ready to go back?" she asked him.

"You bet. I thought I was dead and having an out-of-body experience."

What he said worried her, but there was no time to waste here at the bottom, resolving the mystery.

"Let's get out of here," he said. "This is a place of no return, I think. I'll explain when we're back in the truck."

Chapter 12.

She did not bother with any more questions and ordered the winch to pull them up. The winch pulled and the cable held, hauling them up safely. Minutes later, they were up over the edge. They scrambled to their feet and ran-hopped to the truck, while the winch reeled the cable in.

"We'd better get the hell out of here ASAP!" shouted Deedee.

Arno did not wait for a second invitation and they climbed back into the cab, but they didn't pressurize the cabin.

Even before Arno had taken his seat, Deedee was contacting home base. "RABi, this is surface mission to K204. Deedee calling in, do you copy?" There was no answer, just static. The indicator light was red: no connection to the satellite. "Come on, come on, fly over us!" she demanded of the satellite while looking up, as if she could make it arrive sooner.

"It doesn't look right," said Arno. "It seems as if there is no satellite up there." He called additional commands into the onboard computer, but the results were null.

"We can't wait for the damn thing." She turned on the truck's drive mechanism and made a tight U-turn to return to base. They had barely turned around when she stopped the truck abruptly. "Arno, where is the frickin' road? And the markers?"

The road they had driven on up to this point was no longer. It had vanished. There were no signs of wheel marks, no kilometer and sub-kilometer markers, no road, nothing except pristine lunar soil. Without saying a word, Arno opened the hatch and climbed out on top of the flat bed and then on top of a container. Deedee followed him, climbing next to him, to that high vantage point. They looked around, but they could not locate where the road back to safety was. All they could see was just the desolate lunar landscape, full of mini-craters. Yes, there were tracks made by the vehicle's wheels, but only the U-turn tracks. The road had vanished, and no other wheel marks from their stopping point back to the RABi were visible.

"I'll be," said Arno. "Look at our boot marks."

Only boot prints from the bowl's edge back to the truck were there. Their previous boot marks, from before Arno and Deedee descended into the bowl, were gone, just like the truck's wheel threads.

"I think we are still at the bottom of the bowl and we are either unconscious, delirious, or dying," she said.

"No, Deedee. We are alive. We are on the surface. Although I don't know when." He looked up at the sky.

What she heard startled her. Could this be some kind of posttraumatic effect of the fall? She couldn't know and decided to keep an even closer eye on him. In the meantime, she looked up to see what he was watching, and then she realized what he was searching for. There were no satellites, no points of light moving above, and—worse yet—no recognizable constellations.

She saw an alien sky.

"I think we're on the Moon, but a different moon than the one we arrived here on," he said.

"What do you mean?" She grabbed him by the shoulder unit and turned him toward her. Her eyes were wide with fear.

He sighed and pointed to the bowl behind them. "That hole. It did something to us."

Deedee was not normally the kind of woman who lacked for words, but she was now. She inspected the lunar landscape surrounding them: cold, dark, full of craters, vacuum, and instantly deadly. She extended her gloved hands to Arno, and he took them.

An uneasy feeling of doom descended on her. Nothing is more distressing than being stranded away from Earth, in space or on the Moon, with perhaps only hours to live.

"Are we about to die, Arno?"

Chapter 13.

"Not as long as we have power," said Arno, trying to create a positive spin.

"But that's just for 48 hours, more or less. Once our batteries are depleted, we'll die from asphyxiation." From all the things she had encountered in her space work, this was the closest she'd come to seeing an inevitable death.

"Yes, but we have 48 hours to figure out what to do."

"What happened to you when you fell into the bowl?"

"It's hard to explain. Have you ever experienced a vertigo attack?"

"Sure," she admitted. "After you get spun one too many times in the centrifuge, it's bound to screw up your inner ear. And I felt some dizziness when I entered the bowl."

Arno nodded. "As I was falling in, I experienced a vertigo attack. But not a spatial vertigo attack—I experienced a temporal vertigo."

"What's a temporal vertigo?"

"It's hard to describe, but let me try. As I began falling, I became disoriented, and my sense of time disappeared. I was reliving my life at different stages, as if I were commanding what and when I wanted to experience. Then time stopped, and I was able to get outside my body and observe myself and other people around me. I could move, but everyone else was frozen, as if time had stopped for them. I did it twice, at two different stages of my life."

"Jesus! Time doesn't stop. I think you hallucinated, Arno."

"No, I didn't. I even experienced myself as an old man. It was as if I traveled into the future, being myself, but old. And I willed the time I wished to be in. I even was aware of myself as a boy. It was not a hallucination. I had a temporal vertigo as of when I was then."

"*When* you were? You're in the present. That's all we have. The past is memories, the future is unknown."

"Let me explain it another way. Wherever you are in dimensional space, the location you find yourself in at the moment you recognize it is the present location. It is not possible to see yourself here on the Moon, and in the next instant on a beach in Florida, and in the next skiing down the slopes of Austria. It takes time to travel from one place to another.

"When we travel or walk, we can move forward, backward, or stop, and it all takes time. If we switch space with time, then we can move forward, backward, or stop completely in time. And space behaves according to the direction of time."

"Whaaat? You mean to say that you saw yourself moving backward spatially, walking backward as time was moving backward, like a tape being rewound?"

"No, not walking backward, but I saw myself as a baby back in my mother's uterus."

Deedee was flabbergasted and stared at Arno for a good while. "But you did not inhabit your body. All this happened in your mind. It must have been like watching a movie."

"Only when I stopped the time. I had all the feelings for that moment in time I existed. The feelings as a baby were new, because I didn't remember them. The feelings as an old man were new as well, because I hadn't experienced them yet. But the others I remembered as I experienced them then and now again."

"This is crazy. Major screwed-up crazy." She wanted to walk away but realized they were still standing on a container on top of the truck. Then a thought crossed her mind. "You said you experienced yourself as an old man."

"Yes. Weird, isn't it?"

"But that's good news. It means you'll live to get old and not die here on the Moon. At least *you* won't die here," she whispered the last words.

"That's true. You'd better stick close to me." He made sure he had her hand in his.

Just as he said that, a glint of light appeared near the horizon. While still holding hands, they looked at the new phenomenon. What could that light be? A rescue craft's light beams? No, it was too large, and the light was white and diffuse. They stood on top of the container, staring dumbly at the object that was rising above the horizon.

"That cannot be the Sun," said Arno. "We're seven days away from sunrise."

"It's not as bright as the Sun, and it can't be the Earth, either. We are on the far side of the Moon," Deedee said. "Is it a UFO?"

He did not answer, although a UFO would not be that farfetched in their situation. The object grew to become a white-clouded half-ball, bigger than anything that could be observed from the Moon.

"Deedee, that's the Earth."

"But we are on the far side of the Moon, for Christ's sake!" she shouted. "The Moon does not spin on its axis."

"This moon does, and we're seeing the Earth rising."

"What catastrophe happened while we were in the bowl?" Her chin trembled.

Arno shrugged, as much as he could shrug in his space suit.

The Earth became a full disk as they continued watching it. It was three times as large as the Earth they remembered seeing from the near side of the Moon. It was not a blue ball with whiffs of white clouds, but a white-clouded planet.

"Short of a major cosmic incident . . ." Arno trailed off.

Deedee turned and looked at him with fear.

"We may be on a younger Moon, when it was spinning and closer to Earth as well. A few billion years ago, when the Earth was a snowball."

Chapter 14.

"Jesus! Jesus! Jesus! A younger Moon and a younger Earth?" Deedee made a gesture as if wanting to run her hand through her hair, but her helmet was in the way. "Let's get back in the cab," she said, feeling miserable.

In the cabin they sat silently for a few minutes, contemplating the situation. Because of the time anomaly they were encountering and their immediate dire situation, both of them were perspiring, and the blood pressure indicator in their visors showed high levels. Their air supply depended on the electrical power available from the truck's batteries. Even if they had enough electrical power, once the Sun rose, they would bake and have to drain the batteries even faster to keep themselves cool. And even if they could survive the Sun's heat and find a fresh source of electricity, life in a space suit in a cabin the size of a shower stall would be impossible.

"OK, Arno." Deedee broke the silence, and she punched a button on the onboard computer. "It seems the truck has enough juice to keep us alive for almost three days. That's the good news. The bad news is we'll be dead soon after that. How do we get out of this nightmare and back to our time?"

"I don't have any ideas yet." He raised his arms in defeat.

"What do you think that thing really is?" Deedee pointed to the bowl.

"I was made aware of certain notions that I understood while down there."

"What did you understand, beside seeing your life in reverse?"

Arno made a gesture as if trying to object to what she had just said, perhaps that not all his life was in reverse, but then he reconsidered. "That's not a bowl." Arno pointed to the hole behind them. "It is a temporal hole."

"What is that, a temporal hole?"

"Similar to a black hole, except this one is made of time, not matter and gravity."

She stared at him with wide eyes. "If it is a black time hole, how come we didn't get swallowed up in it and die?"

"Gravity acts on matter, creating black holes. Gravity does not have much influence on time, although it distorts it. Besides, it is not black, as you saw yourself."

"This is crazy," she said. "We fell into it, didn't we? Gravity did that."

"The Moon's gravity did that," said Arno. "The temporal hole has no gravity."

"But something was gushing down that hole."

"That was time, flowing down the hole, influenced by its own physical laws."

"OK, Arno. Tell me what else you discovered while in the Time Hole."

"I fell over the edge because I lost my balance."

Deedee gasped. "And then?"

"After I woke up from my time experience, I was sitting on the path where you found me. To you and me, it looked like a path but, in reality, it is a temporal channel, down which the flow of time travels into that hole to another temporal universe.

"As you know, we live in a space-time universe. We have space freedom—we can move in any direction. But we don't have time freedom. Time has an effect on us, moving in one direction only. Spatially, we can stop or go back, but not in time. The moment is all we have. That thing behind us is where the time we experience flows in and drains away," Arno concluded.

Deedee licked her dry lips. "How long do you think it took you to reach the ledge you stopped on?"

"A lifetime."

"It took you seconds to fall to the bottom. It took me less than 20 seconds to get to the edge and see you contemplating endless time."

"No, it took me a lifetime. Those 20 seconds for you meant over 70 years for me as I was reaching the ledge."

"Holy crap, Arno. Did you age, too?"

"I don't feel older. Remember, I left our time continuum and, while falling, my time was different. I even stopped in time, went back, and then forward. Your timeline was not altered. Only mine."

"Why did you stop where you stopped? Because from that point on, the slope was beginning to steepen sharply."

"I don't know. I don't remember how I stopped, but once there I looked down the hole and tried to make sense of what I experienced and the meaning of time. Next thing I knew, you were yanking me by my shoulder and I heard your voice in my earphone."

"After you fell in, you never heard me? I called you."

"No, nothing."

"Let's go through the timeline. You fell in, and during your fall, you experienced the time anomaly. Then you stopped. Could it be that I stopped you, just by seeing you? By observing you, I might have arrested your fall?"

"It could be," Arno said. "Like observing an electron. Very much like that."

"Definitely, I arrested your slide through the time chute. Then I ran back to the truck, hooked the cable from the winch on my belt, and came after you." Deedee thought for a moment. "Computer, what was the descent time on the winch?" The display showed 202 seconds.

"Could it be that where I found you, we were back in the past, perhaps the past we are experiencing right now?"

Chapter 15.

"Yes," Arno agreed. "I think so. Although it seemed that I slid down in space, in reality I slid back in time, and that spot may correspond to the time we are in right now."

"Then how come the truck, though it remained on the surface, traveled in time with us?"

"The winch cable," he said. "That was the link from the past to the truck in our present, and the truck came back in time with us. If you hadn't been connected by the cable when you came after me and we somehow had managed to climb to the surface, the truck would not have been here."

Deedee shuddered. "Therefore, you fell in, and I followed you to about a few billion years in the past, and now we're experiencing that past moment in time."

They both stared at the big, round Earth above the horizon of a younger Moon.

"That's about it." Arno sighed. "By coming straight back to the surface, as the winch retrieved us, we cut across eons of time, but we stayed in the time you found me at the bottom."

"Oh, my God!" Deedee sighed. "How do we return to our time?"

"I think we can go back to our time, but this is just speculation."

"Even speculation is better than death."

"Very well. We may die anyway, but it's worth a shot. We need to descend back to the place you found me and stay linked to the truck by the winch cable. When we find the original spot, we will have to return along the spiral path up to the rim, and, hopefully, we'll return to our original now."

"If we stay here and do nothing, we're as good as dead. Let's do it." Deedee returned the truck to its original position near the bowl's edge. "Plug in your suit. We need to recharge our batteries."

They recharged their suits, circulated some of their air with air from the truck's tanks, replenished their water, and drained some of the bio-discharges. They had a liquid meal from the truck's supplies before starting.

"There will be some variables," Arno said before exiting. "We need to land at the same time-location you found me."

She ordered the readings from the winch. "OK, I've instructed the winch to take us down at the same rate I originally came down."

"We need to take into account the time it took us to return, the time we spent here on the surface, and the time it will take us to return to the rim. Time is flowing. It does not stand still."

She entered more orders into her computer. "Anything else?"

"The exit point when we return—it could be a variance of years. If we return even ten years earlier, we'll be in no better shape than we are now. No one will be able to rescue us, and we won't be able to return to a RABi that hasn't been built yet."

"I see what you mean. Timing is everything. Could we exit too late, like, in the future?"

"I don't know." Arno pondered. "We'll have to see and wing it as we go." He thought for a moment longer. "Maybe not, because the future hasn't happened yet."

Deedee was puzzled. "But you saw yourself as an old man. That was the future."

"Yes, but that was inside the Time Hole, not out here."

"Then, are you saying that the present is the beginning of time and not when the Big Bang happened?"

"No, the beginning of time was the Big Bang, but soon after, it became the past."

"Wait, wait." Deedee raised her hands. "Are you saying that we create time, as we know it? And that there is no future, but it all starts now and flows in the past?"

"I believe so. There is no future. We imagine it. There is only now and the past."

"If that's true, if we exit out of the Time Hole when the now is, we should be back to our time."

"Yes, I think time falls over the edge in the Time Hole at the time of now."

Chapter 16.

"Have you heard from the K204 mission?" manager Lai demanded from the communication specialist.

"No, nothing," said Martha. "I tried to make contact with them, but there is only silence from the other end."

"Goddammit. Please don't make this another disappearance like Gold Rush," Lai pleaded, looking up. "Sound the alert and get me in touch with the emergency rescue team."

The yellow flashing alert lights were activated only on the top level of the home base. On the lower levels, work continued as usual. Everyone on the top level knew that something bad had happened on the surface, and pre-assigned specialists ran to their stations as instructed by their PCs. One of the crafts was fueled and prepared for rescue, while a second one remained on stand-by. Pilot specialist Randy Hudson and his teammate Hector Garcia were making the final checks before departure. Medics Ashley Paige and Lola Sing shoved their medical gear in the bay area behind the seats, climbed in, and strapped themselves in the middle seats, facing forward. All of them wore space suits, and the interior of the craft was left depressurized and would stay that way in case of rapid action during the rescue. The surface rescue mission team was ready to take off in less than five minutes. The hangar's flat roof split open, allowing the flying potato's three rocket engines to propel the craft to the location where Deedee and Arno were last heard from.

"This is CRAB-A. Pilot specialist Randy Hudson speaking. I'm circling above the last communication site we had with the truck. There is no sign of the truck or the generalists between kilometer markers 131 and 132."

"This is manager Lai. Any sightings of them as you were flying there?"

"Negative. No vehicles on the road."

"Do you see the crater that they supposedly came across?"

"Negative. No such crater exists within two klicks in either direction." The pilot referred to the radius of two kilometers he had inspected around the last known location of the truck.

"Get lower, Randy, and see if you can pick up their wheel tracks on the road."

"Will do." He turned to his co-pilot and said, "One hundred dollars that the tracks continue?"

"You're on," replied Hector.

The craft descended lower for the pilots to distinguish between old tracks and the K204 mission's tracks.

"What the hell!" Randy exclaimed. "The tracks end in the middle of the frickin' road."

"They sure do. Heh, heh, heh." Hector snickered as he watched the magnified tracks on his monitor. "An easy hundred bucks."

"Manager Lai, this is Randy. The tracks end abruptly."

"What? Land and do a visual inspection of the road. Make sure your rocket exhausts don't blow the evidence away."

"Roger that," responded Randy.

Back at RABi, Lai was perspiring nervously. All he needed now was an investigation team from Earth. "Damn it," he whispered.

Hector pointed to a small mound 30 yards from the road, and Randy approached the spot. The craft's three engines were mounted high, one in the rear and the other two laterally on the front, to reduce blowing dust when landing. The three engines rotated to a complete vertical position and Randy got the craft to touch down softly on its sled rails.

"Alright. Ashley and Lola get on the ground and approach the road only on pristine ground. Hector and I will get out on the other side of the road, and then the four of us will do a visual search of those tracks from both sides of the road."

"Roger that," said Ashley. She and Lola stepped outside on the lunar soil. They didn't bother with their emergency medical gear since there weren't any victims in sight. Yet.

A short time later, Randy landed the craft across the road at a safe distance, and he and Hector approached the road on foot.

There were about seven meters between the two search parties, with the road in the middle. They walked along the road, video-recording and searching for the mysteriously disappeared wheel tracks.

"Manager Lai. This is Randy. We'll open a conf link so you can see and hear what's going on."

"Roger, Randy."

"Also, you'll see two sets of images, one from the left side of the road from Lola's camera, and from Hector's on the right side."

"Roger that. Just don't step on any evidence."

"We'll be careful," acknowledged Randy.

The two teams walked cautiously along the road, following the truck's treads. They stopped when the tracks ended.

"The truck stopped here first," said Ashley, moving her light closer to the ground to detect the deeper impression of the wheels as they came to a stop.

"Yes, and after that it seems they continued at a lower speed," said Randy. The wheel marks were clearly imprinted deeper in the dust, so the speed must have been very slow at that point.

"Here, they stopped again," said Randy.

"About nine or ten meters from the last stop," said Lola.

"And they stopped again, and that's where the wheel tracks end," said Ashley. "It seems they approached whatever they saw very cautiously."

"I think they saw whatever they said they were seeing," agreed Hector.

"There are two sets of boot marks, one large and the other smaller," said Randy. "Matches Arno and Deedee's sizes. It seems they walked about 20 meters, stopped, and turned around, facing the truck, and then that's where they end."

"Deedee's marks indicate that after going to the same spot she returned," said Hector this time. "She was running back to the truck—look at the span of her footsteps—and she slides to a stop. Then she returns back to where Arno's tracks disappear, and her boot marks disappear as well."

"Were they together when their boot tracks disappeared?" Manager Lai asked.

"Can't tell if they were together, or if Arno went first or Deedee, or if Arno waited for Deedee to return from the truck," said Randy. "Both sets of their boot marks are side by side and facing the truck when they cease to exist."

Chapter 17

"Any other boot marks in the vicinity?" manager Lai asked.

"No, theirs are the only ones, besides old wheel tracks," said Randy. "No one walked around here except them, and now us."

"What are your scanners reading?" manager Lai asked.

"Radiation typical for this part of the Moon," said Lola. "There are no other energy or radio emissions."

"There are no infrared signatures of any kind, except for us," added Hector. "Even Deedee and Arno's boot marks are cold."

The four lunar rescuers stood on the side of the road, gawking at the footprints. Hector even looked up, as if looking for an unidentified lunar flying object.

Lola remarked, "Didn't they say they saw a large crater, like a bowl?"

"Yes, that's what they said in their last communication," said Randy. "Round and smooth, and blue-green."

"What if they were seeing a flying saucer and mistook it for a bowl?" asked Hector. "Maybe a ULFO and aliens kidnapped them. Plucked them right from the road."

"And I'll pluck you if you don't stop spreading false rumors," said Lai on the common channel.

"Manager Lai. This is Randy. It looks as if they've disappeared into thin air, or vacuum. Almost as if they came across a Bermuda Triangle here on the Moon."

"What are you talking about?" Lai's voice trembled from fear or anger.

"Manager Lai, I'm looking at the 3-D scanning of the boot marks. The only place Deedee, Arno, and the truck could have disappeared to would be upward. But there are no signs of rocket exhaust, either."

"I don't think they went up," said Lola. "Look at the heel marks. They are deeper, as if they leaned backward. Maybe there was a crater and they fell in it."

"If there was a crater here, where is it?" Hector asked.

"Even if it was here, in which direction did it open up?" Ashley asked.

"That way, where the boot marks disappear," Randy said, pointing in the direction where their boot marks were no more.

"Both of them fell backward," Hector said.

"What the hell?" That was all Lai could utter. "Again, is there any evidence of a crater?"

"No, nothing," said Randy. "The road and old wheel tracks continue to the horizon."

"Which is not that far," added Hector.

"Manager Lai, I changed the resolution, and it seems that there are marks of a rope among the footprints," said Lola.

"The plot thickens," Hector said. "Is that the mark of a cable? Right there in front where the truck stopped. That could be the winch cable." He used a red laser beam to indicate the spot.

"It is," confirmed Lola. "Right among the marks of the rope, but only there, in that spot."

"Why would they use the rope and the cable?" wondered Hector.

"To descend into the crater," said Randy.

"I didn't authorize them to explore the inside of the crater," shouted Lai.

"Well, that's what the marks indicate. They went down inside something that doesn't exist anymore," said Randy.

"Is the terrain solid around you? Undisturbed?" manager Lai asked.

The four specialists looked around. Then Lola and Hector scanned the nearby soil.

"Manager Lai, we're standing at the point where the boot marks disappeared," said Randy. "If there were a rim here, we, or at least I, should be standing with one foot in the crater."

"No sign of soil alteration," said Lola, and she walked ahead along the road.

"It is as solid as ever," confirmed Hector, and he walked parallel to Lola.

"Hey, don't venture too far!" yelled Randy.

"What happened, Randy?" shouted Lai.

"We're OK. We're standing on solid ground," said Hector, and he crossed the road to the other side to Lola.

"Manager Lai, Hector and Lola walked along the road, and Hector even crossed the road, and they're still there," said Randy. "Nothing happened. There is no crater or whatever."

"OK, here is what I want you to do," said Lai. "Make a perimeter around the area before the truck stopped the first time and after the boot marks ended. Place a blinker on the road at both ends to alert any future vehicles not to drive over it."

"Roger that," acknowledged Randy. "Hector, Lola, Ashley, use rocks to demarcate the area. I'll retrieve the blinkers."

He returned with the devices, which he implanted on the road, and he activated their lights. Each blinker had a small solar panel on top for recharging during daylight. The other three finished placing the rocks and stood by for further instructions.

"Manager Lai, we're finished here," said Randy.

"Randy, before returning to base, search and scan the area on a wider diameter."

"Roger that. Randy out."

Chapter 18.

Arno and Deedee reached the end of their descent into the Time Hole, or at least based on the previous descent plus some educated guess-time added to it, and looked around. Nothing indicated that they had returned to the same spot where or when they had been before.

"Can you make out if we're in the right place?" Deedee asked.

"No, nothing, it looks the same." Arno looked up at the helical rings of flowing time. "Although we need to be in the right time, the same time we left, place doesn't mean anything here."

"Then this time is as good as any. Shall we walk up the path of time?"

"I suppose you want me to go first," said Arno.

Deedee waved her arm for him to get started. He walked up with great effort, as if he were climbing a very steep slope or going against a strong current, or something else not ever encountered before.

"This is very difficult," he said. He looked up to where the cable ended over the rim. "Maybe I'm pulling against the cable."

Deedee ordered the cable to slacken as they were moving along the path away from the cable's origin. Although Arno was in front of her, she, too, felt opposition from something. They were both affected by the flow of the time current.

Slowly, placing one foot in front of the other, while slackening or tensing the cable as needed, they made progress toward the rim. As the helical paths increased in diameter they felt less resistance, and at certain points they even used the winch to help their progress.

"Why do you think it's getting easier the closer we get to the rim?" Deedee asked.

"Maybe the pressure of time diminishes as we go to the now moment."

"I hope you're right about the now moment, when we'll exit. We didn't account for this extra time and energy it's taking us to reach the rim."

"No, we didn't. Now I'm worried if we have enough power and clean recycled water," said Arno.

"We have to make it. We're almost halfway up."

Arno climbed over the edge first and pulled Deedee up to the surface. They stood still for a moment, catching their breath and taking the last sip of water from their SLS tanks. It had not been easy walking up against the flow of time, and they felt exhausted. The truck was in sight, which was good news. The power level in their suits was down to a half-hour. Quickly, they approached the truck and unlatched the winch cable from their belts.

"The climb took a toll on my legs," said Deedee.

"Same here," agreed Arno. "I checked the CO_2 in my suit and the level is normal, so it must have been the climb against time."

"It had to be. Let's get in the cabin and recharge."

After they were back inside, they closed the hatch, pressurized the cabin, and removed their helmets. Their faces were wet with perspiration, and it felt somehow easier to breathe without their helmets on, which was just a state of mind.

"It's good to be back home," said Arno.

Deedee gave a small yelp. "Look, Arno! There is the green light for satellite connection. We're back in our time."

They hooted and embraced each other. Indeed, it was good to be back home.

"RABi, this is surface mission to K204, do you copy?" called Deedee after their enthusiasm abated.

There was only silence at the other end, punctuated only by occasional static. Deedee repeated her call several times, but to no avail.

"Now what?" Deedee said, exasperated.

"I can see the satellite up there," said Arno. "RABi, this is surface mission to K204. This is generalist Arno Bacher. Do you copy?" There was only silence. "Goddammit!" Arno cursed in frustration.

They could hear faint garbled communications coming from the speaker. Both of them perked up their ears. The volume increased, but the words were truncated, making it very difficult to understand what was being said or even if the communication was in English.

A few seconds later the communication became somewhat clearer and they heard, "..ret...er...aft...o..rt... an...ne..."

Deedee called on her mic enthusiastically, "RABi, this is surface mission to K204! This is generalist Dolores Da Villa. Do you copy?"

They listened but no one responded. She repeated the call, but the garble they heard before continued, unrecognizable and fainter. Moments later, there was only silence.

Deedee and Arno looked at each other with desperate eyes.

"When are we, Arno?"

"Hell if I know, but at least we are sometime in modern times. Look, we can see the road we came on." He pointed out the wheels tracks on the road and the kilometer markers.

They both looked at the road ending in the blue-green bowl. Without another word, Deedee pushed the joystick in reverse and distanced the truck from that hole, then made a tight U-turn and accelerated back to RABi.

Chapter 19.

RABi's transmission tower's red light blinked above the horizon. Their hopes rose, and minutes later the aboveground facilities appeared in their entire splendor, which now did not resemble dilapidated buildings in the California desert anymore but sublime architecture. All that was missing was a smoking chimney to welcome them home.

"RABi, this is surface mission to K204 returning to base. This is generalist Arno Bacher. Do you copy?" Nothing but silence greeted them. "We should be communicating directly with the tower. What's going on?"

"I don't care, I'm driving in," said Deedee as she drove the truck into the corrugated metal tube tunnel leading to garage #4. The door was wide open and they drove inside.

Arno was the first to get out and call for the dispatch, with no luck. He even jumped up and down and waved his arms at the garage camera, but no one responded.

"Are we invisible?" wondered Deedee, joining him.

"What's going on? Are they in the conference room eating the leftover donuts and not paying attention to the monitors?"

"Let's get in." She walked to the hatch, plugged in the intercom link, and commanded the hatch to depressurize and let them in, but nothing happened.

Arno looked at Deedee, and without a word he opened the control panel on the wall and entered manual commands to open the hatch. The display on the panel indicated that the airlock was being readied for access, and 30 seconds later they opened the hatch and stepped inside. Voice commands were useless, so Deedee accessed the control panel inside the chamber and manually activated the pressurization. In 15 seconds the pressure was equalized with the inside of RABi. Arno unlocked and opened the hatch, stepping inside the station.

"Arno, keep your space suit pressurized."

"You bet. God knows what's happening inside here."

They got out into the empty corridor and assessed the situation. The hatches to the other airlocks were closed, which was normal. So far, so good. He looked at the atmosphere display on the wall; the readings were normal.

"Nobody is here to greet us," said Arno.

"Let's go to the central offices." Deedee began walking determinedly in that direction.

Samir was at the dispatch desk, busy updating some records, when he looked up at the monitors. Something caught his eye. Garage #4 wasn't empty. The truck sent on the K204 mission was there. Unoccupied. He stood up, disbelieving what he was seeing. They were conducting a search for them outside, and here they were, inside the base.

Without delay he ran to manager Lai's office. "They–
they're here," he said, pointing in the direction of the
garages.

"Who's here?" Lai asked.

"Come and see, sir, on the monitor." Samir ran out,
pointing to the screen.

Lai joined him, but the monitor showed an empty
garage.

"What are you talking about?"

"I saw the truck in the garage. It was there. I swear
on Vishnu, it was there. Maybe it went out again. The
garage hatch is still open." Samir punched a few
buttons and the monitor displayed the empty exit to
the surface. The monitor displaying the surface did
not show a truck, either.

"Are you losing your mind, Samir?"

"I saw the truck. It was there!" shouted a
hyperventilating Samir.

"Did you happen to see the generalists as well?" Lai
asked.

Samir shook his head.

Manager Lai returned to his office and dropped in
his chair, shaking his head. He opened the com with
the rescue party. "K204 mission rescue party, this is
manager Lai, do you copy?"

"This is the rescue party. This is Randy."

"Any sign of them?"

"Negative. We've spiraled out to 5 clicks and so far,
from the point of incident and the outer perimeter,

there are no signs of them. We have only 20 minutes of fuel. Request to return to base."

"Acknowledged and approved," said Lai. "Randy, return to base while following the road. Fly low, look for fresh wheel marks."

"Roger that, but the most recent marks were left by the K204 mission truck leaving RABi."

"Follow the road, just in case. Manager Lai out."

Deedee and Arno came into the central corridor, and a specialist in a blue jumpsuit passed by without acknowledging them. They were dressed in space suits, and anyone would have found it unusual for someone to be suited at this spot in the compound.

"Hey!" Arno shouted, but to no avail. Besides, his helmet was sealed. "Did you see that, Deedee?"

"Yeah. She passed us as if we didn't exist," said Deedee.

"What the hell is going on?" Arno unsealed his helmet and pulled it back. He inhaled and said, "It's OK. Same stale air as when we left."

Seeing that Arno was fine, Deedee did the same. "At least we can see and hear each other without the use of the radio."

"I hear someone else coming our way," said Arno.

Coming from the opposite direction, a generalist and a specialist were discussing a smelter's technical problem.

Arno stood against the wall opposite Deedee and when the two passed between them, Arno said, "Hello, John. It's me, Arno."

Neither one acknowledged their presence or even flinched. Specialist John was either deaf or couldn't hear Arno.

"Mary!" yelled Deedee from behind. They continued walking without paying any attention to her call. Deedee didn't give up. She ran after them and caught Mary by the elbow. But a strange thing happened: Her hand slipped off Mary's sleeve as if it were oiled. Deedee stopped and looked at her hand, unsure of what had just happened.

"Weren't you able to grab her?" Arno asked.

"No. It seems they don't hear us or feel us. I felt her, but it was as if there was no friction. Her sleeve was slippery as grease." Deedee stared at him, dumbfounded. "What do you think is happening?"

"Not sure. We can hear and see them. Originally, I thought the radios didn't work, but when we shout at people walking by and they don't hear us or see us, that's troublesome."

"Aftereffects of the Time Hole?"

"What else? Let's visit the offices." Arno turned around, and Deedee walked quickly to catch up with him.

"What if we can't communicate with them?" she asked.

"We'll figure out a way."

Samir was uneasy. He kept looking at the monitor, hoping to see the truck again. An empty garage was all he saw. As he turned his eyes to the computer monitor on his desk, he saw a glint of two people outside the office's glass wall. The images were faint, but they quickly became stronger and stronger. They were Deedee and Arno, out there in space suits without their helmets on, waving their arms. He stood up and raised his hand to wave at them, but their image began to disintegrate into vertical bands, as if they were behind evenly spaced bars. The bands became thinner and thinner until Deedee and Arno were gone.

Chapter 20.

Arno and Deedee saw Samir and waved to him. He turned white. His mouth gaped open, and he stood up, raising his hand as if to wave at them.

"Arno, he can see us!"

Both of them waved their arms back at him. Finally, they were visible!

But he didn't wave back at them and his eyes became as wide as full moons. He looked disturbed.

"What's going on?" Arno impatiently shouted, "Hey, Samir, can you hear us?"

"Let's get in," said Deedee and she rushed through the nearby door, followed by Arno.

Once inside, they flanked Samir, who at first was motionless, but then he slowly raised his hands and smoothed his sleek black hair, which had been standing up on end.

"Did we scare you, Samir?" asked Arno.

"Dear Vishnu!" he exclaimed and ran to Lai's office without responding.

"I think he saw us, but now we are nonexistent again," said Arno.

"Let's follow him," said Deedee.

The door to Lai's office was left open and they walked in. Samir, his hands propped on Lai's desk, was talking to him, while Lai looked at him with his arms crossed.

"I'm telling you, I saw Deedee and Arno. They appeared and then disappeared in a strange sort of way." Samir pointed to the outside.

Lai stood up, pushing his chair back. "Where did you see them?"

"Outside in the corridor. In their space suits." He pointed to the clear plastic wall separating the offices from the tunnel.

Lai looked out to the corridor. "I don't see anything. Are you hallucinating?"

Samir collapsed on a chair in front of Lai's desk.

"Martha, did you see anything strange in the corridor?" Lai asked through his com.

"Like what, strange?"

"Like Deedee and Arno?"

"Really? Where?"

Arno and Deedee could see Martha up on her feet in front of the com-center, observing the corridor through the glass wall.

"I guess you didn't see them," Lai said.

"You mean they've been rescued? They're back?"

"No. Samir thinks he saw them, but maybe it's only his imagination." Manager Lai looked at Samir and said, "Maybe you should go to the infirmary."

"Sir, I'm not mad. They are here."

"But only you saw them and their transport. After you talked to me about the garage, I sent a specialist to check it out. It's empty."

Samir exhaled loudly. "Then I saw ghosts?"

Seeing Samir was distraught, Lai thought it would be wise to have him elaborate. "Tell me what and how you saw them."

"I–I looked up from the monitor and saw Arno and Deedee standing in front of the glass wall. They looked a little dim at first, but then they became real, as real as you and me. They were waving at me. Then they became striated—a set of lines appeared in front of them. And those lines became wider until they disappeared and I could see only the wall behind them."

"Those lines you say you saw, were they vertical bars?"

"No, no, come to think of it, those lines were the background, the wall behind them. It was like their images were sliced vertically and the wall behind them occupied the gaps."

"Like one of those effects you do on an overhead presentation when you move from one slide to another and the image fades out through vertical slots?" Lai asked.

"Yes, yes, something like that."

"And you saw them in their space suits?"

Samir nodded. "But without their helmets mounted."

"I don't know what you saw, but your desire to see this situation resolved and not have Earth come here to investigate and snoop on us made you see things." Lai waved his arms to make his point.

Samir stood up, dejected. Half-believing Lai, he returned to his desk.

"What do you think, Arno, are we ghosts?"

Arno reached over and took Deedee's hand. "I can feel you."

"So do I. We must be made of solid matter." Deedee walked to Lai's desk and sat on it. She waved her hand in front of his eyes, but he did not even blink. She then placed both of her gloved hands on either side of his face and rubbed it. "He's slick—no friction whatsoever."

Lai stared outside, keeping an eye on Samir.

"Let me try this." Arno removed his space gloves. He walked behind Lai's chair, grabbed him by the shoulders, and tried to push him sideways. His hands slipped right off the manager's jumpsuit material, as if it were made of satin. "There is no friction."

Deedee picked a framed picture off the wall behind Lai. "Look—I can lift it without any problem."

"Maybe this phenomenon is not applicable to inert, nonbiological objects," said Arno. "Let's see what Lai does if I kick his chair."

But just as he was about to do that, Samir burst into the office and closed the door behind him. Without saying a word, he walked to the window and closed the blinds.

"What's the matter?" Lai asked.

"Check the recent records on garage #4 airlock access." Samir turned the monitor halfway to be able to see as well. Lai punched in the request, and Deedee and Arno bunched together on the other side to see the information on the screen.

"What the hell is this?" wondered Lai.

"That's right. The airlock was activated manually ten minutes ago. From the outside with someone using Arno's access code and from inside with someone using Deedee's code."

Arno and Deedee looked at each other. Finally, there was a way to be acknowledged.

"Do you believe me now?" Samir asked.

"If they are alive, they could be in another realm," said Lai.

Samir nodded. "They and the truck occasionally appear in ours."

"The nonexistent crater may have been real to them. And somehow they returned."

"We need to bring them back, before outsiders come investigating."

"We have time, three months before the next transport. We'll figure something out," Lai said.

"What's going on?" wondered Arno. "Why are they worried about investigations from Earth if they don't find us?"

"Hmm, that's a good point. They may be afraid that the investigators will talk to the workers here and something unsavory will be discovered," said Deedee. "I suspect these two are smuggling something."

"Do you know if gold or diamonds were discovered in any of the mines?"

Chapter 21.

"Not around here," said Deedee. "Diamonds and gold are two things we haven't discovered in Racah crater. Yet."

"We'd better find the other component before the investigation starts," Samir demanded, standing up and placing a finger on Lai's desk.

"Don't use that tone of voice with me, Butala," Lai objected.

"Outside your office you're my boss, but here we are partners, Bo," said Samir. "Don't let your position go to your head. I represent my government in this mission. Who do you represent, some Chinese billionaire?"

"Keep your voice down," said Bo Lai. "Let's talk to Vieyra and see what progress he's made."

"The plot thickens," said Arno. "Samir is an agent of the Indian DAI, and Bo is working for a billionaire, no doubt a front for the Chinese MSS."

"And the Brazilians have Davi Vieyra working for ABIN," concluded Deedee. "What are they trying to find and smuggle to Earth?"

"Something important," said Arno. "Let's listen."

"Martha, connect me with Vieyra at K204, please," said Lai on the intercom.

After a few seconds, the green light on the intercom flickered.

"Davi, are you there?" Lai asked.

"Yeah, I'm here," said Davi Vieyra, not too cheerily.

"Samir is with me, and we need to talk," said Lai.

"Samir, where are my compressors?" Davi asked.

"Didn't you hear?" Samir said in rebuke.

"Hear what, about your rescue search? What does that have to do with my compressors?"

"Your compressors were on the truck we lost," answered Samir.

"Crap!" Davi replied. "I'm not sure how long this compressor will last. Do you have another one to send me?"

"We may have a bigger problem than that," said Lai.

"Like what?"

"If we don't rescue the two generalists, we'll face an investigation from Earth," said Lai.

"You should have flown the damn thing, Samir."

"That was not my decision," responded Samir.

"Hey, I made that decision to keep a low profile on the whole situation," said Lai.

"Well, now it's got a high profile," replied Davi.

"Let's be professional about this," Lai said. "What's the situation over there at S18?"

"I haven't found it yet, and I need a new compressor to dig deeper."

"Why are you wearing the compressors out so fast?" Lai asked.

"I don't know, but shortly after we discovered the first pole and gave it to you for safekeeping at RABi, the compressors began breaking down. The first one that broke had been working since K204 was started five years ago. Now they don't last more than a few weeks."

"And you think that the new compressor will last longer than the others?"

"Like I said, I need it to dig deeper to find the other pole," said Davi.

"I never understood why you're not using electrical drills." Samir said.

"Because they don't work. The pole interferes with the electric motors. I have to use closed loop pneumatics," explained Davi. "This happened in other mines where the magnetic fields were also strong."

"Davi, can you guess what makes the compressors fail?" Lai asked.

"Unlike other mines, the magnetic fields don't exist here. I think the problem is caused by the damn poles."

"Since when did you come to that conclusion?" asked Samir.

"Since about now. There isn't any other explanation. The pole or the poles are the problem."

Chapter 22.

"What poles are they talking about?" Arno asked Deedee.

"I don't know," she replied. "Whatever these crooks are doing, for now, it's not our concern. We need to get back to our time."

"For sure." Arno contemplated opening the door and leaving.

"Davi, did the compressors break down before you discovered the first pole?" Lai asked.

"I don't think so, Bo. They began breaking down after I sent you the first one."

"We have only one compressor left in stock," said Samir. "If the last one dies, then what do we do?"

"Bring back to K204 the other pole," Vieyra said. "Along with the last compressor."

"Would that be wise?" Lai wondered. "Remember what happened to some of the miners."

"We'll keep it away from S18," replied Vieyra.

"OK, I'll fly to K204 with the compressor and the pole," said Lai.

"No. We will fly together," Samir said.

Lai was not happy but he conceded. "Then you go and fetch the compressor, and I'll get the pole."

"The pole is right behind you in the safe," said Samir, pointing to the wall.

"Yeah, yeah, I'll get it. Go get the compressor."

"No, you get the pole out of the safe now and send someone else to fetch the compressor," said Samir, narrowing his eyes.

"I'll have to get the craft ready. If we split our efforts, we'll get to K204 sooner," said Lai.

"I don't think you're going to get here any sooner if you continue arguing," Vieyra said over the intercom.

"Call Randy and tell him to ready the craft," said Samir to Lai. "You're dragging your feet, Bo. Open the safe and let's see the pole."

Lai sighed. "Well, it is not in the safe."

"What?" Samir and Vieyra asked in unison.

"Don't panic. I moved it for safekeeping to another place. In the farthest greenhouse, L22."

"And why did you do that, Bo Lai?" Samir stood up.

"Because it affected me. I began experiencing the same symptoms as the miners at S18."

"When did you move it?" Samir insisted.

"Just recently."

"You're a liar, you son of a bitch." Samir pinned Lai with murderous eyes.

"Hey, stop arguing!" Vieyra shouted over the intercom. "Get the damn pole and the compressor and come here quick."

"Sit down, Samir. Vieyra, we'll see you in less than an hour." Lai disconnected and contacted Randy. "Randy, are you back?"

"We just arrived, manager Lai. Sorry we couldn't find any trace of them or that mysterious crater."

"You did the best you and your team could," said Lai.

Deedee and Arno exchanged shocked looks.

"They went to rescue us and we had disappeared," lamented Deedee.

"And the bowl as well," said Arno.

"I have another mission for you right away," Lai told Randy.

"I need to refuel. Where are we going?" Randy asked.

"To K204. Is the other craft, CRAB-B, fueled?"

"Yes, but Hector is at the end of his shift," said Randy.

"We don't need to take Hector," Lai said.

"But that's against the rules," objected Randy.

"I'm a certified pilot. I'll be the second pilot. Stand by the craft. We'll have a compressor delivered."

"Who else is coming?"

"Samir Butala."

"The dispatcher?"

"Yes, and stop asking useless questions. Have the craft ready by the time we get there. Over and out."

Lai and Samir left the office in a hurry.

Chapter 23.

"Amazing what you can find out when you're invisible," Arno said.

"Just a bunch of crooks," said Deedee. "Didn't you find Samir's description of our apparition puzzling?"

"Lai thinks that we're in another realm," said Arno.

"Well, aren't we? In another time realm?"

"Well, the space dimensions are the same, and our time is not faster or slower than theirs. The Time Hole did something to us, but what?"

"Yes, the universal clock moves with the same speed for them and us. But if it moves at the same speed, why are we invisible, then visible, and why do we then vanish after a short time?" Deedee wondered.

"Samir said he saw us appear dimly and then take full shape, becoming real. Why didn't we dim out and vanish, just like we appeared?"

"Yes, why did our image become striated?" added Deedee. "The effect of light, do you think?"

"You mean as seen through a slit," said Arno. "But we're not a photon acting like a wave."

"Our image could be scattered when projected through a slit."

"But we would have multiple images, ranging from faint to strong. What Samir described is a vertical segmentation, as if we were out of synch."

"Out of synch? Like how, Arno?"

He perched on Lai's desk, thinking. "It almost sounds like a frequency aberration."

"I don't follow you."

"Have you ever seen an incandescent electric bulb powered by AC captured at high speed?"

Deedee shook her head.

"When you capture the image of a bulb at high speed and then play the images back at normal speed, the bulb becomes luminous and then it dims, going through that cycle at the frequency of the AC. The case I saw once was using 60 Hertz, and the light pulsed at 60 times per second."

Deedee raised her eyebrows. "I still don't get it. We're not bulbs powered by AC electricity."

"No, of course not. But we have a frequency, and it may be a different frequency than the world around us."

"You mean like heartbeats?"

"No." Arno shook his head. "Let me explain it this way. Frequency is space flowing through time. In the case of the bulb, it was the frequency of the electricity, which was nothing else but the rotations of the rotor in a generator between the magnets per second of time. Space over time."

"OK." Deedee nodded.

"What if our time and space flipped? The space flows now, while time can stand still or move. Instead of cycles over a period of time, like a second, we were transformed to project time units per a constant movement of space."

"Flip space and time. You said you were in a realm where time could stand still or go backward when you were in the Hole. Could that be the effect?"

"Mh-hm."

"Then how will we be able to change back this anomaly of reversed roles of time and space?" Deedee shook her head, distressed at being stuck where they were.

"It is just speculation. We cannot explain why we fade in and striate out. And why it doesn't happen more frequently."

"According to Samir, he saw the truck appear as well. Maybe the phases between apparitions are longer."

"Could be, and we may appear again," agreed Arno.

"Darn it," said Deedee. "The crater, the Time Hole, disappeared as well."

Arno glanced at a topographical map of the Racah crater and its vicinity posted on the wall. "The Time Hole was located after we passed kilometer 131, wasn't it?"

"I think so," said Deedee.

Arno walked to the map and placed his finger on the yellow line designating the road between RABi and K204 at the kilometer marker 131. "I need a straight edge."

"What for?" questioned Deedee while looking for a straight edge in the office. "How about a string?" Deedee pointed to a roll of nylon string on a cabinet.

"That's even better," said Arno. He pulled a tack from a corkboard and inserted it at marker 131, or close to that point. He made a loop on the string and, using it as a chord, he extended it to RABi. Holding the string at that point he moved the string in an arc to the location of K204.

Deedee yelped in surprise. "Arno, the Time Hole was located exactly at the midway distance between the two camps."

"How about that?" said Arno, satisfied with his finding. "Although we were at kilometer 131 by road distance that was the middle point between the two stations, as the lunar crow flies."

"Which happens to intersect the road at that very point," concluded Deedee. "What does that mean?"

"I don't know. But now, according to the rescue party, it's not there anymore."

"Maybe we made a mistake," said Deedee. "We should have stayed near the hole and waited for the rescue party."

"And what if they couldn't see us, just as it's happening now?"

"At least we were near the hole," said Deedee.

"What if the hole became visible to us, just as we became momentarily visible to Samir?" Arno asked. "Once we went in, we became part of it. For some reason, the hole disappeared and then the rescue party couldn't see it. I bet the hole is still there."

"Speculations, that's all we have." Deedee grabbed the rings of her SLS as if grabbing onto suspenders, thinking. "On the other hand, if we need to get back there, why drive? We can fly."

"The craft needs fuel," said Arno. "We don't have the codes to refuel the craft in hangar A."

"But we have fuel," said Deedee.

Arno grinned. "The truck. That's right."

They left Lai's office in a hurry, heading for garage #4.

Chapter 24.

Martha's inquisitive eyes followed Lai and Samir as they rushed out the door. She had had Lai's office bugged and so she had listened in on the conversation with Vieyra. This was the first time she heard the poles being mentioned by that name. Usually it was "the component." And now they were taking it back to K204. She knew Lai was working for the Chinese and Samir for the Indian intelligence services, but Vieyra was new in this plot. He must have been working for the Brazilians. All they needed was a Russian and they could call themselves the BRIC secret agent team. But there was no Russian involved in this, as far as she could tell. There weren't any Russians at RABi at all. Of course, the Russians could use Bulgarians or Serbians, their usual minions, and there were a few of them here and at K204.

This mysterious pole turned out to be two of them. She was told to keep an eye on Lai and Samir, because they were about to smuggle a rare element found at K204, S18. What exactly were these poles? At least one of them had affected the minds of the miners at S18, and Lai said it had affected him as well, as his justification for taking the poles to greenhouse L22. The two secret agents, who didn't seem to trust each other much, were on their way to K204 by rocket craft, but for what reason? Besides the compressor, why did Vieyra need the pole back? Her assignment was to monitor the communications of Lai and Samir, not to follow them. Someone from her agency was assigned to intercept them at K204.

To her surprise, Martha saw Lai's office door open all by itself. Soon after, she saw Arno and Deedee exiting into the corridor. They were faint images and they wore space suits. "What do you know?" she thought, "Samir was right—they are alive." She hurried after them and as Deedee and Arno rushed down the corridor, they became better defined, more visible. She ran after them and was about to shout at them when their images became striated. That stopped her in her tracks; she'd never seen anything like that. But Samir had said something similar about them. The last residual slits turned around the corner, and she ran after them with renewed vigor, but they were gone by the time she reached the corner. There were several bifurcations in the corridors and without having seen where they went, it was futile to go anywhere.

Back at her desk, she checked the monitors and saw manager Lai and Samir in their space suits exiting to the surface and heading on a rover to the greenhouses, which were dark during the lunar night. On another monitor, in hangar B, Randy was loading the compressor on the haul tray under the belly of the craft.

"Randy, do you copy? This is Martha," she called into the mic of the com-center.

"Yes, what's up, Martha?" answered Randy.

"Do you have a manifest for what you're loading on the craft?"

"I haven't seen one, but this is a new compressor for K204. Remember, the ones we sent earlier did not make it," replied Randy. "Why are you asking?"

"Well, I'm doubling for Samir, who's left his desk."

"That's right," acknowledged Randy. "We all have to wear multiple hats here."

"Is there an emergency at K204?"

"I don't know, but Lai told me to take the compressor along with him and Samir, of all people, to K204, pronto. Do you know why Samir is coming along?"

"Hey, I'm just a mushroom. Have a safe flight, Randy. Martha out."

Lai, holding a cylindrical aluminum case, and Samir boarded the craft. The hangar's roof slid open and the craft took off upward.

Martha didn't waste another moment and opened a secure channel. "Easy, this is Lurker. Do you copy?"

"Roger, Lurker," responded a man with a gravelly voice.

"Have a satellite follow craft CRAB-B, which just took off from RABi and is on its way to K204. Lai and Butala have the component, and it is referred as a pole. Repeat p-o-l-e. Davi Vieyra is in cahoots with them, and he's digging for another one of these poles at S18."

"Roger that. Easy out."

Martha had to maintain her image as a diligent worker, so she connected with Samir. "Samir, do you copy? Martha here."

"Samir here. What's up, Martha?"

"You left your desk unattended. Do you want me to cover for you?"

"That would be great, Martha. Thanks."

Chapter 25.

Arno and Deedee used the manual codes for the airlock and entered the garage where they had left the truck. As they passed the trailer, Arno patted the round spheres containing the rocket fuel.

"How much fuel is there?" Deedee asked.

"Plenty to get us even to the International Space Station around Earth, if we needed to."

"How are we going to pump the fuel into the craft's tanks?" Deedee squeezed in the truck's cabin, followed by Arno.

"There will be hoses there," Arno said as he shifted the truck into drive.

Out they went, cutting across the dusty field toward hangar A, where the CRAB-A craft was parked. As they approached the hangars, CRAB-B rocketed up toward K204.

"There they go," said Deedee. "They could have done this in the first place and not have jeopardized our lives."

Arno just nodded and he maneuvered the truck inside hangar A alongside the rocket craft. Deedee climbed into the cockpit to check its status. Arno took the job of fueling the craft.

"Hey, good news," said Deedee. "Randy hooked up the umbilical to the craft and it's ready. Oxygen, batteries, and ancillaries are all good."

"Excellent," responded Arno from outside. "I'll decouple the hoses from the base supply tanks and couple them to our tanks, then I'll connect the hoses to the craft. We'll use the crafts pumps to suck the fuel in." Arno glanced at the two capsule-shaped tanks on the roof of the craft.

"Make sure you connect the right hose to the right port. I'm not ready for heaven yet."

Intermixing the compounds in the tanks meant an instant explosion, as the two fuels would react violently when combined.

"Don't worry, the hoses and the ports are idiot-proof," said Arno.

It didn't take long to fuel the craft and disconnect the hoses and the umbilical. Arno climbed into the cockpit, where he found a frustrated Deedee.

"What's the matter?" he asked.

"This frickin' thing needs a pass code."

"You've got to be kidding me. In case of emergency, how are you supposed to fly the craft?"

"Emergency be damned!" Deedee flipped through the instruction images for flying the craft. "Even the instructions say to enter the pass code."

"Enter 'resume'," Arno said. "Maybe we can use Randy's last flight access."

Deedee did as instructed, but she got a red warning message. "We're stuck."

"Are you certified to fly this craft?" Arno asked.

Deedee gave him a frustrated look. "Of course I am. Are you?"

"Sure am. You need to enter your license number. That's the code."

"Ohh…I don't remember it."

"I do mine." Arno keyed in his code. The access screen turned green. "Punch it, Deedee."

"No way, Jose." Deedee pointed up. "The roof is closed."

Arno craned his neck looking through the ceiling window at the closed roof above. "Open it."

"I tried. It needs a code as well," said Deedee, giving up.

"In that case, we'll have to fly horizontally out of the hangar," said Arno. "I'll take over."

"How are you going to do that?"

"I'll use the three main rockets to lift us off the deck, and then I'll use the altitude control rockets, the ACR, to slide out." He flashed her a reassuring smile.

Arno fired the three rockets, two located laterally in front and one in the rear, and gingerly lifted the craft off the hard floor, after which he used the ACR in the rear to exit the hangar.

"We're clear," said Deedee.

Arno rotated the main rockets toward a more horizontal orientation and blasted away.

Martha's mouth gaped open when she saw CRAB-A exit from hangar A and then disappear upward.

Chapter 26.

Martha's mouth opened even wider when she saw the truck, which allegedly was lost, parked in hangar A. She blinked and rubbed her eyes, but the truck was there. She considered her next action: sound an alarm to inspect the truck or call the agency. She didn't have to think about it for too long, because the truck disappeared soon after.

"What the hell is going on?" she murmured to herself. She accessed the flight status for the craft, which had Arno's code.

"CRAB-A, you are not authorized to fly. Please respond. Who's on board?" Martha listened but there was no response. "Screw this." She had better things to do. She immediately opened a secure channel. "Easy, this is Lurker. Do you copy?"

A second later she heard the gravelly voice, "Roger, Lurker."

"Something bizarre is going on here at RABi. Craft CRAB-A just launched away from here heading in a northerly direction, most likely toward K204."

"Who's in the craft?"

"Arnold Bacher, science generalist. And very likely Dolores Da Villa, engineer generalist."

"Did they have authorization to leave?"

"Not that I know of. But that's not the bizarre part. Arno and Deedee, that's what we call them, disappeared on a mission to K204 about 11 hours ago."

"Please elaborate, Lurker."

"They were sent by ground to take supplies to K204. At marker 131.2, they called in reporting a crater in the road. Soon after that we lost contact with them. The rescue team did not find the truck or the generalists, and they didn't see any crater in the road. The crater was reported to be in the shape of a bowl or a dish antenna."

"What?"

"That's right, but there's more. I saw the two of them here at RABi for a moment, and then poof, they disappeared. After CRAB-A took off, their truck, which was lost as well, became visible in hangar A. I saw it but it, too, disappeared soon after."

"Are you saying they're invisible?"

"Something weird like that. They shift in and out. What do you think?"

"Why are you reporting this? Does it have to do with Lai and Butala?"

"I think Samir Butala has seen them, too. He told Lai, who asked me if I'd seen them. At that time, I hadn't. Soon after that, Butala and Lai took off for K204."

"Is there a connection?" Easy asked.

"My senses tell me that there is something unusual going on here," said Martha.

"OK. Check on the truck, and I'll get the satellite to follow CRAB-A to its destination. Easy out."

Martha looked at the security desk, but no one was manning the post. She was all alone in the main office.

She shivered with uneasiness. Although a seasoned agent, never had she dealt with apparitions before—and on the Moon, of all places.

"Security, do you copy?" Martha called.

"Umberto Zarco speaking. What's up, Martha?"

"Umberto, where the hell are you? Did you know that craft CRAB-A took off from hangar A?"

"Say what? I didn't know of any clearance for it to fly." Umberto was quiet for a moment as he checked his PC. "Arno Bacher? Wasn't he missing?"

"Yes, but he entered the code and flew away. Or someone used his code. Listen, you need to go out there to the hangar and check it out. Call Hector Garcia and get him involved as well. The craft didn't have fuel. See what's going on."

"Will do. Umberto out."

Martha wiped her brow. These recent events were beyond weird. She'd overheard Randy saying the craft was out of fuel. She checked the fueling station access codes, but no one had used them since Randy had landed. Where did they get the fuel?

Ten minutes later, Umberto Zarco entered hangar A.

"Umberto, this is Martha. What do you see?"

"An empty hangar. And two disconnected fuel hoses on the deck."

"They are not connected to the fuel station?"

"Negative."

"Do you see any wheel marks?"

Umberto walked around, looking at the ground. "It's a hard floor, there are no marks."

Martha looked at one of the monitors and saw Hector walking toward the hangar exit airlock. "Thanks, Umberto. Hector will join you shortly. Please assist him." She pulled up the manifest for the K204 mission, and there it was. It had carried rocket fuel as well.

"Easy, this is Lurker. Do you copy?"

"Roger, Lurker."

"Arno and Deedee used fuel from the truck, which they were transporting to K204. The truck is nowhere in the hangar. The two are on CRAB-A. Are you tracking them?"

"Oh yes, but they aren't going to K204."

Chapter 27.

CRAB-A achieved its parabolic trajectory, heading toward marker 131. The onboard computer cut off the engines, flying ballistically.

"Do you think we can correct all this when we find the hole?" Deedee asked.

"I hope so. The Time Hole caused our frequency distortion, and the solution lies in it."

"How are we going in and out? We don't have the truck and the winch," said Deedee.

"We have the craft and its winch," replied Arno, pointing down to where the winch was located under the belly of the craft. "If we feel frisky, we might pilot the craft into the hole." Arno saw Deedee's terrified face. "Maybe not."

"What are we going to do when we get there?"

"I have a simple theory, which may scare you. We get in and out."

"That does scare me."

"I said it's simple. Look, I first went in and then you followed, and both of us got out together. We've been in and out twice, but only once starting from our real time and back to the real time. The parameters of our frequency were reversed at that time. I think that if we go in and come out again, we may reverse it back to normal. And we may not have to go all the way to the bottom, just a few feet in. I hope."

"That's it?"

"That's all I can think of. On the other hand, the phenomenon may wear out and we will be back to normal anyway."

"Pray for a miracle," Deedee concluded.

The engines fired up to start their descent. Arno took control from the computer and piloted the craft to marker 131.2. Hovering over that spot, he and Deedee looked eagerly for the Time Hole. There wasn't any sign of what they thought they would find.

"It's true. The hole has disappeared," said Deedee. "Get lower."

Arno piloted the craft as close as possible to the fine powdered ground without blowing away any tracks. They could see the ring of rocks made by the rescue team earlier, but nothing else.

"Let's land there," said Arno, pointing to a spot near the road, where the rescue craft had landed earlier.

They disembarked the craft and walked straight to where their boot marks ended when they had fallen into the Time Hole.

"Nothing, just the Moon," said Deedee.

"Let's take a walk," said Arno as he continued along the road, with Deedee trailing behind.

"There's no use, Arno, it's not here." Deedee pointed to their boot marks left from the previous time. "Maybe the bowl started and ended exactly where our boots were visible that last time."

"The Time Hole opened in zero space?" wondered Arno. "Then why did we see it? What triggered its opening?"

They continued walking along the road, but there wasn't any Time Hole or depression they could see, just the road. Heading back slowly along the road without talking, they stopped at the boot marks they had left when they went into the bowl. There was nothing beyond their heel marks. No Time Hole.

"Remember when you used that string on the map in Lai's office?" Deedee asked.

"This spot was the midway point," said Arno. "But where? Here, there..." his voice trailed off. "I think the midpoint is where our heels left the last imprint." Arno walked and placed his boot heels exactly in the same spot, but the Time Hole did not appear.

"Something else triggered the opening of the Time Hole then," said Deedee. "That something is gone. Or if this is the exact midpoint between RABi and K204, then that something shifted." Deedee stopped analyzing the situation. "Arno, we've got to go to K204."

"Why?"

"Woman's intuition."

Chapter 28.

Arno took the controls of the craft and *floored* it. "Tell me about your intuition."

"Something Lai said. He moved the pole from his safe to the greenhouse, because it affected him," said Deedee.

"Yes, yes, I see what you're saying. The poles. The midway between those two mysterious poles caused the Time Hole. We came across the Time Hole when one of the poles was in Lai's safe. During our return to RABi and before the rescue team arrived, he moved the pole to the farthest greenhouse at RABi. How far do you think that is? Two kilometers?"

"Something like that," said Deedee. "But the rescue team would have seen the Time Hole if it had moved only by two klicks."

"True." Arno thought for a moment. "But what if the other pole moved as well at S18?"

"We're speculating," said Deedee.

"Maybe, maybe not. Vieyra said they were having problems finding the other pole. What if it shifted position as well?" asked Arno. "We need to go to S18, not K204."

Deedee nodded in agreement and reached to change the flight parameters toward S18, which was three kilometers west of K204.

"Don't," said Arno, stopping her. "They are tracking our transponder. Let's go to K204, circle around it low to the ground, and approach S18 at ground level.

Some of the mine shafts and leftover minerals there might confuse the transponder tracking us."

"Good plan." Deedee smiled at him. "Big and smart."

"Easy, this is Lurker. Do you copy?"

"Roger, Lurker," the gravelly voice responded.

"We're trying to contact CRAB-A but no one responds. I'd give it another five minutes before we need to alert Earth. Where is the craft?"

"It went to the place where the truck mission got lost, and now they're on their way to K204."

"Do you have people in place?"

"It's taken care of. Easy out."

Martha felt she had done her job for right now. The action was to be at K204, or maybe S18.

"Martha!" shouted Umberto, back at his security post two desks away. "CRAB-A is heading for K204, after they stopped at marker 131.2. You'd better alert K204 about the rogue craft. Do you want me to contact Earth?"

"I'll contact Earth as well. Thanks, Umberto," said Martha. She wasn't going to inform K204 or Lai about the rogue craft just yet. And Earth had to be kept in the dark for right now. What would Lai and his co-conspirators do if they heard that the craft, possibly piloted by Arno, was coming their way? Better to keep them in the dark.

"Umberto, how long until CRAB-A reaches K204?"

"At their current speed, four minutes."

"Thanks. Hey, is all the evidence secure at hangar A?"

"Yes, I think so. Why?"

"How about the exit to the hangar?"

"What do you mean?"

"What if whoever stole the craft had inside accomplices?" Martha asked.

"Oh shoot, you're right. I'd better change the codes."

"Better yet, why don't you padlock the exit?"

"Thanks, Martha." He hurried out to secure the exit to the hangars.

Good—now she could take her sweet time without being bugged by Umberto.

"K204, this RABi. Do you copy?" Martha opened the communication.

"Roger, this is K204."

"Hey, I'm looking for manager Lai."

"Manager Lai? Isn't he at RABi?"

"No, he flew to your place, K204."

"Hold on, RABi."

Martha examined her nails. At smaller mining stations, the janitor was the communication specialist, among other things, and competence was in short supply.

"RABi, manager Lai is at S18."

"K204, get me in touch with Samir Butala."

"Who?"

"Samir Butala, K204."

"Hold on, RABi." A moment later, "Someone here tells me that he is with manager Lai."

"Man, you seem to be overworked there," said Martha with as much compassion as she could fake.

"If you only knew..." And without any more encouragement the communication specialist, who didn't bother identifying himself, gave Martha an earful. Martha sympathized with him by interjecting occasionally the customary "uh-huh."

Martha looked at the time on her monitor. CRAB-A was almost there.

"That sounds really awful, but can I talk to Davi Vieyra?" Martha asked.

"Hold on, RABi."

This guy was on something, thought Martha. All the information was or should have been on his console.

"RABi, supervisor Vieyra is with the people from your place."

"K204, where are they again?" Martha asked. To her surprise she was placed on hold again until she got the answer she already knew. "Thanks, K204. Martha out."

She opened the secure com. "Easy, this is Lurker. Do you copy?"

"Roger, Lurker."

"As you may know, CRAB-A may be at K204. Lai, Butala, and Vieyra went to S18."

"Roger that. We lost track of CRAB-A near K204."

"What?"

"No, they didn't crash. The electromagnetism there is bad and it interferes with the signal."

"Easy, I don't know what's going on at K204, but one guy I spoke to seems to be stoned or something."

"I don't understand."

"Vieyra and Lai mentioned that the poles affected people's minds. I hope your agent is in the right state of mind."

There was a pause. "I'll have to look into that."

"I think CRAB-A will be landing near S18," said Martha.

"Why do you think the two generalists are going there?"

"A gut feeling."

"Do they know something I don't know?"

"I'll go out on a limb here, but since they seem to be invisible, there's a good chance they overheard the conversation in Lai's office."

"What proof do you have?"

"The door to Lai's office opening and closing by itself."

Chapter 29.

Martha realized that she hadn't gotten in touch with Lai yet. She had to cover her tracks.

"K204, this is RABi. Do you copy?" said Martha.

"Roger, this is K204." It was the same guy.

"Listen, I need to get in touch with manager Lai."

"Who?"

And the entire conversation repeated.

"Pipe me in to S18. Can you do that?" Martha's job was to drag her feet, and the guy at the other end was a cooperating dullard. Not surprisingly, the communication to S18 didn't happen.

Martha drummed her fingers on her desk. She had to inform Earth. But first she had to inform the manager, trying one more time to get in touch with Lai. Protocol dictated that. She connected via satellite to S18, directly to Lai's com.

"Manager Lai. This is RABi. Do you copy?"

"Roger, RABi. This is manager Lai."

"Manager Lai, this is Martha. We have a situation here."

"Hold on." Lai sealed his helmet for a private discussion. "What's the problem?"

"Craft CRAB-A was flown away without authorization."

"What? Who piloted it?"

"Arno Bacher's code was used to fly the craft from the hangar."

"Where did he go?"

"Security tracked him to K204."

"Here? Why here?"

"Manager Lai, I wouldn't know that."

"Sonofabitch," mumbled Lai.

"Do you want me to inform Earth?"

"Uhh...no. Wait until I get to the bottom of this. Repeat, do not inform Earth. Who from RABi is missing?"

"Hold on." Martha opened the screen showing every worker's whereabouts, or rather his or her PC's location. "Manager Lai, only you, Samir, Randy, Arno, and Deedee are absent from RABi."

"Thanks. Manager Lai out."

Martha reclined in her chair, smiling. What was Lai up to? Could be he worried about someone else at RABi maybe knowing about his thievery and coming to K204?

"Well, did you inform Earth?" Umberto entered the office after completing his task.

"No. Lai said to wait."

"Can he do that? Only a director has that power. He can't do that."

"He is the acting director, remember?"

"Hmm," grunted Umberto. "Well, everything is locked down. Although with no crafts here, no one can go anywhere."

Lai considered his options. He had the pole in the aluminum case. Samir and Vieyra didn't know about the other craft. And who was in the other craft? Arno was missing and only Samir supposedly had seen him and Deedee. Could they be alive and coming here? Did they know about the poles? Who were they working for? He didn't have answers for these questions, and it troubled him.

The other problem at hand was finding the other pole, buried somewhere in one of S18's shafts. And when they found the other pole, he needed to get both of them away from here. Because of some unfortunate circumstances, he had had to ally himself with the Indian and the Brazilian. He didn't know what exactly these two poles were, but General Li had told him that whichever nation possessed these two poles would be the most powerful on Earth. And he intended to make China that nation.

He looked at the aluminum case, which was the size of a cylindrical lunch box, on the table in front of him. Any compass's north pole went crazy, pointing at it, when it was near it, while the south pole of a magnet would move away from it, no matter what orientation. Whatever that element was—if it even was an element—it was very precious.

Samir stared at Lai suspiciously, seeing him with his helmet sealed.

What were his plans? Lai wondered. If Arno and Deedee were on the craft coming here, were they working with Samir? Of course. Samir is the one who selected Deedee and Arno for the mission to K204. Why didn't he see that before? Lai needed to take action, so he unsealed his helmet.

"Where is Vieyra?" Lai asked the assistant specialist in the office.

"Supervisor Vieyra is in shaft 89.4/6. But he's returning here."

Lai stood up. "I need to go to the bathroom." He had to do something else and not make Samir overly suspicious.

"You're in your space suit," said Samir.

"I need to empty my bag," Lai said. "Keep an eye on the lunch box."

That was good enough for Samir. He didn't want to lose sight of the container with the pole.

When Lai was outside, he contacted Randy. "Randy, this is manager Lai. Do you copy?"

"Randy here."

"What's your location?"

"K204. The lunch room."

"Randy, is your craft parked outside?"

"Yes, I can see it on the monitor. Why?"

"Is there any other craft out there?"

"No. What's going on?" Randy asked.

"I just received a call from RABi. The other craft was hijacked and is heading for K204."

"No way! Do you know who hijacked it?"

"Not sure, but Arno Bacher's code was used to fly it away."

"Arno? But he's missing."

"Maybe, maybe not. I want you to find CRAB-A. It must have landed near K204 by now. Arrest the hijackers."

"Right away. Randy out."

Chapter 30.

Arno steered the craft in a low circle around the K204 base, and then, just a meter above the lunar soil, approached S18. He landed behind a large boulder just 50 meters from the muffin-shaped shack that was the entrance to the S18 mine.

"Ready?" Arno asked Deedee.

"As ready as I can be," she replied.

"Do you think they have weapons in this craft?"

Deedee shook her head as she placed her helmet on. She opened communication with Arno and said, "We're invisible. That's our weapon."

They exited the craft and approached on foot. They didn't know if S18 had exterior cameras or if someone was watching and had detected their craft, although it was behind the large boulder. Outside the entrance shack, there were several lunar rovers, and two lunar haul trucks were parked near the discharge mouth of the mine. It didn't take long to reach the entrance airlock after they walked, needlessly, as stealthy as they could under the lunar darkness.

"Should we ring the bell?" Deedee asked and then added, "Sorry, I forgot we don't exist."

"Well, you're the engineer—figure out how to access the airlock."

"Arno Bacher, don't you know that coming from outside you don't need a code?" Deedee accessed the manual lock and the hatch opened, letting them in.

She pushed the pressurization button and observed the pressure gauge rise and the green light turn on to access the mining station. However, getting from the airlock to inside the mine's upper level required a code, and neither Deedee's nor Arno's codes worked.

Arno inserted his comm link in the console to contact someone inside, but no one answered. "I keep forgetting that they can't hear us, either," said Arno. "Even pounding on the hatch won't do any good."

"Might as well make ourselves comfortable and wait for someone to access the airlock." Deedee slid down to a sitting position near the hatch leading inside.

Randy boarded his craft and initiated the tracking system, but nothing blipped. He engaged the rockets and hovered over the K204 complex. A small bleep appeared near the S18 mineshaft and he followed it, arriving quickly over the CRAB-A craft. Without wasting any more fuel, he landed next to it. The other craft was dark, but his infrared sensors saw the rocket nozzles were still hot.

He reached the hatch of the other craft, plugged in his link on the exterior control panel, and energized the craft. The interior camera showed an empty cockpit. There was no one inside and on the outside only his boot marks were visible. Could this craft have been navigated remotely? He checked the status of the recent flight and it showed a pilot using Arno's code had operated the craft.

"Manager Lai. This is Randy, do you copy?"

Manager Lai, sitting across the table from Samir, heard Randy in his earpiece and answered, "Roger that. Report."

"CRAB-A is parked outside the entrance of S18. There is no one onboard."

"Lock it down."

"Roger that."

"Join us. Manager Lai out."

"What was that?" inquired Samir.

"I asked Randy to join us," Lai answered.

Samir did not have a chance to ask any more questions because Vieyra came in with a big grin on his face.

"We found it."

Samir and Lai shifted their eyes to the specialist sitting nearby. Vieyra understood and said, "Gomez, why don't you take a coffee break?"

Gomez didn't wait for a second invitation and exited the room.

"Well?" Samir said.

"The darn thing migrated," said Vieyra. "That's why we couldn't locate it precisely and snake after it. It migrated again, getting closer to a major shaft, and my man snake-drilled in and captured it."

"That's great news, Davi," said Lai. "Bring it here. There is room in this case for its brother." Lai patted the shiny container.

"Are you out of your mind, Lai?" Vieyra looked at him sternly. "What if these two components are matter and antimatter?"

"We don't know that," Lai said.

"No, we don't, but I don't want to be de-atomized, either," said Vieyra.

"Nonsense. They seem to possess some kind of polarity aberration."

"We don't place them together. We don't know what we have here," Samir piped up.

"Absolutely. And I happen to have a similar container in which to store it," said Vieyra.

"So you'll keep the other component," Lai said.

"That will keep us honest." Vieyra smiled coldly.

"Well, there are two components, and there are three of us," said Lai. "Who's going with which component?"

"I know who you are and what you have with you," said Samir. "I'll go with Davi."

The two men got up and exited, leaving behind a sour-looking Lai.

Chapter 31.

Deedee and Arno observed the red alarm light blinking and the pressure gauge dropping, warning of depressurization. Someone seeking access from outside was depressurizing the airlock. A few seconds later, the hatch opened and Randy stepped inside. After closing the hatch, he pressurized the airlock, without giving any indication that he was aware of the other two. Once the green light turned on, he opened the hatch and stumbled back as if a gust of air had entered the airlock. Deedee and Arno had rushed out ahead of him into the mine compound. Unperturbed, Randy entered into the mine.

"Let's follow him," said Deedee.

Ahead of them in the corridor a door opened, and Samir and Vieyra came out. They didn't pay attention to Randy and walked away.

Arno ran to the door and spotted Lai inside. "Deedee, I'll follow them. You stay with Lai." He pointed to the room and with long strides he took after Samir and Vieyra.

Randy opened the same door, and Deedee saw Lai inside. She squeezed in between Randy and the door and took account of the room they were in. There was no one else but Lai and Randy in a room that functioned as a com center, dispatch, and monitoring for that particular mine station.

Lai sealed his helmet. "Are you armed, Randy?" he asked.

"Of course," said Randy, patting his side zipped pocket. "Do you expect trouble with the hijackers?"

"Possibly. Stay alert, and follow me and my orders." Lai watched the diagram on a control monitor and placed a finger on a particular shaft. "We're going there."

Deedee, in her space suit, didn't have access to their com and couldn't hear what was said. But after seeing their tense faces and both of them suited up for a vacuum as well, she expected trouble down in the mineshaft. As soon as they exited, she got out, too, and followed them closely.

Arno caught up with Samir and Vieyra. They didn't speak but stopped at a locker, and Davi removed a shiny aluminum container, after which both of them sealed their helmets. Arno figured they were either going to the surface or into the mines, and he followed them closely. Neither one of them knew that an invisible Arno was standing with them in the airlock and later in the elevator that descended deep below.

The elevator stopped at the lowest level, and after exiting into a dark chamber, Samir and Vieyra turned their shoulder lights on. The descending tunnel they took was narrow and low, and at times Arno had to walk hunched over behind them. He couldn't hear their conversation, but he understood their intention and followed closely, making sure he didn't step, roll his boot on the pneumatic hoses that powered the drills in the shafts and fall down.

After waiting for the elevator to come up, Deedee sneaked in with Randy and Lai and took the ride down. She wondered where Arno was, and she hoped that she would not become visible any time soon. They exited at the bottom and she kept close behind Lai and Randy, following them down a tunnel into the mine.

Samir and Vieyra arrived into a small chamber, where a miner sat motionless on a rock. Near him, the pneumatic "roto-rooter" snake-drill stood idle. Arno observed the miner looking mesmerized at an object in his gloved palm. The other two gathered around the miner and bent over to see up close the mysterious pole. Arno managed to look between the two.

A small sphere resembling mercury levitated above the miner's palm. The sphere was about a centimeter in diameter, and over its gray-silvery surface occasional flashes traveled slowly. That was the component, or the pole. A drop of mercury? Arno couldn't make sense of what he was seeing. Maybe that wasn't mercury. Through his goggles at a magnified setting the sphere had a black aura around it, like soot, that was barely visible from farther away. He had never seen anything like it. A new element, perhaps? The sphere rippled, even changing slightly its shape but then re-forming itself into a sphere again, as if it were liquid metal. Maybe it was mercury. But at the low temperature of -100⁰C in the mine, the mercury should be frozen solid.

Vieyra opened the case and invited the miner to drop the sphere in. Surprisingly, the miner refused and kept on staring at the ball. Vieyra gave the container to Samir and retrieved the pneumatic drill. Arno couldn't believe what happened next.

In cold blood, Vieyra activated the tool and bored it into the miner's body, under his armpit. The miner leaned back against the rock wall, the inside of his helmet splattered with blood gurgling from his mouth, only his hands twitching as he died. Vieyra dropped the tool, took back the container from Samir—who seemed to be as stunned as Arno was—caught the sphere in the container, and shut it close.

"Did you have to do that?" Samir shouted.

"Mining accidents happen," said Vieyra. "Unfortunate but necessary. I don't know how this ball, this component, makes people lose their minds. The container will protect us for a while. Let's go and reunite it with its other half."

"Not so fast." Lai, accompanied by Randy, stood a few feet away in the tunnel.

"Why did you come down here?" Vieyra asked. "This could be dangerous, bringing the case with the other component."

"And as you see, nothing has happened. No boom." Manager Lai bent slightly sideways to see the dead miner on the ground. "I see we have our first casualty over these poles."

"A mining accident," said Vieyra.

"Peculiar mining accident," commented Lai.

"Arno, what the hell happened here?" Deedee spoke over their com from behind Lai and Randy.

Arno was bent down, examining the almost-dead miner. He hadn't noticed the two new arrivals. Hearing Deedee, he looked her way. "Deedee, what are you doing here?"

"I followed them down here. Who killed the miner?"

"Vieyra. The miner wouldn't give the sphere away."

"What sphere?"

"The component, the pole. It is a sphere of mercury, for all I could assess. Oh yes, and it levitates."

"Since when does mercury levitate?"

"Maybe it was a nut," said Arno.

"Arno, are you OK?"

"I think I just experienced a temporal vertigo. I think the sphere caused it." Arno stared at the container Vieyra was holding and then at Lai's container.

"What's the matter?" she asked.

"Look, do you see it?" Arno pointed to something between the two parties.

Deedee focused and felt her mouth open. "Holy shit, Arno. There is a tiny Time Hole between us."

The blue-green shape of the top half of an hourglass floated midway between the containers.

Chapter 32.

"Who cares about a dead miner? We have both components now," said Vieyra.

"Let's get out of here," Samir said.

"Sure, but I want the other case first," said Lai. "That is the property of IUM."

"Oh, yeah?" Vieyra bent down and picked up the pneumatic snake-drill.

"Since when are you a company man?" Samir asked.

"Company man, my ass," Vieyra said between gritted teeth. He stood behind Samir. "Lai, you'd better walk slowly toward me and give me the other component. I will keep both of them." Vieyra raised the snake-drill with its sharp, barbed bit.

"Don't be stupid. What are you going to do with that tool?" Lai laughed nervously.

"I'm surprised, you being a manager, that you don't know how deadly a snake-drill is. Bring me the case or you're dead."

"Randy, shoot that criminal," Lai ordered.

Before Randy could unzip his pocket to reach for his gun, Vieyra unleashed the snake-drill. Lai moved quickly out of its way. The diamond-tipped drill, turning at high RPMs and trailed by the flexible snake, hit Randy in the chest. The drill wormed through the SLS vest and the suit, but before it went through Randy, Vieyra retrieved the snake. Randy was still fumbling for the gun in his pocket when he dropped to his knees. Air, particles of machinery, pieces of suit material, and blood erupted from Randy's SLS vest. Randy managed to pull his gun out before he fell flat on his face on the ground. Quickly, Lai grabbed the small aluminum revolver from his hand.

Deedee, standing behind Randy and Lai, screamed when she saw the atrocious crime committed.

"Don't lose your wits, Deedee," said Arno, breathing heavily. "Lay low, just in case we, too, are caught in their squabble."

"Oh, God. Oh, God. What are we going to do, Arno?"

"Nothing for now. Lai has one pole and the gun. Vieyra has the other pole and the snake-drill. Samir is in the middle, and he's got nothing."

"Don't let them kill Samir," said Deedee.

"Why, you want to kill him yourself? The sonofabitch is the one who caused us this problem."

"I didn't mean it. Arno, I'm afraid one of them will kill Samir."

"I think we have a stalemate," Lai said to Vieyra. "I've got one pole. You have the other. I have a gun. You have a snake-drill, which you know how to use. And then there's Samir, who's empty-handed."

"Two poles, two weapons, and three men," Vieyra said. "How should we solve this, Samir?"

"I urge you not to make any rash decisions, gentlemen. There will be consequences. I may not be armed and I may not have a pole, but my government will take severe actions against the survivors. Besides, neither one of you can afford to kill me, as the other will kill my killer."

"Hmm, he's got a point, Lai," said Vieyra. "If I bore him, you'll shoot me. If you shoot him, I'll bore you. But neither one of us has a use for Samir."

Deedee was desperate to find a solution to this impending tragedy. As she lay low, one of her boots rolled onto a hose. "Arno, disconnect the pneumatic hose."

"But then Lai will shoot the other two."

"So we're going to watch and let them kill each other? What am I saying? You're right—Lai would win and the others would be dead."

"Not much else we can do. We can get out of here and whatever happens, happens."

"And the Time Hole. We need to access the Time Hole," said Deedee.

"We're stuck, just as they are stuck."

"You know, we can't stay here forever," said Samir. "Someone will come looking for us. Why don't we abide by our original agreement, ironed out by our governments, and walk out of here alive?"

"You're full of good ideas, Samir," said Vieyra. "But that's all you have, good ideas to save your brown ass. We cannot walk out of here together. Lai's got a gun, and I won't drop the drill."

"He's right, and I'm blocking the exit," said Lai. "I think I have all the advantages. Drop the drill and give me the other pole, Davi. I'll walk out of here and let both of you live."

Vieyra laughed mockingly. "You take us for fools, Lai. You know what our governments do to failures and traitors?"

Samir was looking back and forth, from one to the other, when suddenly something caught his eye. "What is that?"

"What is what?" Lai asked.

"That." Samir pointed to something in the air. "That."

"Is this another trick of yours, Samir?" Vieyra asked.

Lai saw it. "What the hell is that?"

"What the hell are you talking about?" Vieyra shouted.

"That blue-green funnel." Samir squatted down, pointing to the Time Hole.

"Bullshit, there's nothing th—" Vieyra then saw the hazy shape levitating in the tunnel between them.

But that was the last thing he saw as Samir yanked the pneumatic hose, knocking Vieyra down.

Chapter 33.

Quicker than anyone could imagine, the calm, methodical Samir, squatting low, had the drill pointing at Lai.

"Shit, you're as quick as a snake," said Lai, raising the gun higher.

"More like a cobra," Samir smirked. "Don't underestimate an Indian." Without taking his eyes from Lai, Samir reached over and picked up the container with the pole from Vieira's gloved hand.

Lai looked intently over Samir's shoulder, as if seeing something. "How are you going to deal with Davi behind you?"

"Good try at bluffing," said Samir. "Vieyra is dead. I slashed his pant leg and cut him. My blade was coated with synthetic cobra venom, one hundred times more deadly than the real venom. He's dead." Samir gave a sinister laugh, showing the narrow blade that protruded from the back of his glove.

"Is Vieyra dead?" Deedee asked from behind Lai.

"If he's not dead, he will be soon," replied Arno, bending over him. "His suit leg has been slashed open. He's losing blood and air. I don't think he's breathing anymore. He's dead."

"How could that happen?"

"Samir did it. Who knew he was this deadly?"

"OK, Arno, let's get the hell out of here. Let them kill each other."

Arno considered her words. "I don't want to lose track of the poles and the Time Hole. How about we both walk into it and hopefully restore our timeline?"

"But then we'll become visible and mortal. Those two will kill us, too."

"Yeah. The darn hole is in between them, and who knows how they'll react when we appear."

"You're right, Samir. We cannot stay here forever," Lai said. "I'm leaving."

He walked backward slowly, but Samir pulled the trigger and the snake-drill went through Lai like a harpoon. Lai stopped momentarily but then ran toward Samir and discharged all his bullets into him, collapsing on top of him.

Deedee screamed and dropped down to her knees. Arno looked in disbelief at Lai, face down on top of Samir, both of them dead. Blood and air were spurting out through Lai's back along the drill protruding out of the SLS vest. A streak of fizzing blood gushed from under Samir, which quickly evaporated or froze. His eyes were still open.

Arno ran to Deedee and lifted her up to her feet. "It's over. They're both dead."

"Why did Samir shoot Lai? He was backing out of here." She was crying and shaking.

"Samir figured that Lai would have punctured the air hoses, and he wouldn't have a weapon anymore," said Arno, holding her in his arms. "Then Lai would have come back and shot Samir, and the poles would have been Lai's."

Deedee stopped crying, staring at Arno. "What do we do now?"

"Let's retrieve the containers with the poles."

They walked to where Lai was on top of Samir and pulled them apart. Lai dropped his container, but Samir still held onto his. Arno wrested the container from Samir, and Deedee picked up the other one from the ground.

She opened the container and looked inside. "All these deaths for whatever this is." The sphere in her container was a ball of mercury, as Arno said, with a black sheen. "Arno, does this look like a galaxy?" She pointed to the sphere, where a miniature spiral galaxy glittered inside it.

Arno took a step back, opened his container, and looked at the sphere. "A beautiful spiral galaxy?"

"Are these real?" Deedee wondered.

"We don't know what these things are. My galaxy is a clockwise spiral."

"Mine is counterclockwise," she said. "My inner visor compass points to it, indicating north."

"My compass indicates south. How could this be? We're side by side." Arno turned the container around and thought for a moment. "That's why they called them poles. These spheres are unipolar."

"That's impossible." Deedee turned her container around. The compass's electronic North Pole in her visor continued pointing to the container and the sphere. "Magnetic poles cannot be separated, yet my sphere is always north."

"And mine's always the south pole. Let's close the containers and check to see if they form the Time Hole again." Arno placed his container on the ground.

Deedee stepped away a few feet and placed her container on the ground as well. Between the two, a small Time Hole formed. She picked up her container and moved farther away. The Time Hole increased in size.

"Now what are we going to do?" she asked.

"What we wanted to do all along—walk into the hole."

They walked toward the hole and held hands, while the Time Hole swirled lazily between them.

"Now!" said Arno, and they embraced.

"Did…did it work?" asked Deedee, looking around.

She and Arno moved apart. The Time Hole was swirling in between them as if nothing had happened.

"Yes," said Arno. "Yes, we're back."

"How do you know?"

"Listen, we can hear the mining's radio communications."

Deedee was about to jump on Arno with joy, but he kept her at arm's length and moved away from the Time Hole.

"Now we can," he said and took Deedee in his arms.

They even kissed. That is, they kissed the inside of their soft helmets as they pressed their mouths together. Each one left lip imprints inside the helmets. Deedee was jumping in place and bumped her helmet into the tunnel's ceiling a few times.

"Let's get out of here," Arno said as he picked up one of the containers.

Deedee picked up the other one and they turned to walk out, when they saw a newcomer with a big gun pointed at them.

"Stop right there!" the man ordered.

Deedee and Arno froze. The man approached, stepping over Randy's body. He saw the other three bodies in a pile at the end of the tunnel.

"Who are you?" Arno asked.

The man approached, pointing the gun barrel at Arno. He then inserted his link into Arno's shoulder port, after which he pulled it out and inserted it into Deedee's port.

"Now we can talk. I encrypted our transmissions. I'm Gomez. You have the poles?"

Arno and Deedee lifted the two containers to show him.

"Who are you with?" Arno asked.

"I'm Gomez."

Chapter 34.

"Keep holding on to the canisters," he told them, and he passed them to inspect and video the dead foreign agents. After he'd done his job, he returned and said, "Time to go." He motioned to exit the chamber.

Deedee was first, followed by Arno, while Gomez was behind them. He let them hold the two containers, unafraid that they may try to destroy the poles, even if that were possible. At the elevator two others, a man and a woman dressed in space suits with no identifiable logos, motioned for them to step into the elevator. The two lifted a red cylinder, not much different than a large fire extinguisher, except for the red lights blinking on a panel, and went inside the mine.

"Our job is done here," Gomez said as he pushed the "up" button. As they were ascending, Gomez communicated with other parties, probably reporting what he had seen.

Arno and Deedee had no choice but to do as Gomez ordered. If he was a special agent, which no doubt he was, it was futile to fight him. Arno considered activating the Time Hole to become invisible again. As if Deedee had read his mind, she looked at him and shook her head. For now they'd take their chances with Gomez and whoever waited for them at the top.

They reached the top level, which was deserted. Gomez escorted them out through the airlock to the outside. Nearby, a new craft was waiting for them, and they were asked to climb in. This was a larger flying potato than RABi's crafts parked nearby. Besides the pilots' two seats upfront, the craft had eight other seats, with two rows of three seats each in the middle, facing each other, and one last row of two seats in the back. Gomez pointed for them to sit down in the middle row facing forward, which they did, after giving Gomez the two containers with the poles. After stowing the containers, he sat opposite them next to the only other person in the craft.

"Hello, Deedee and Arno. I'm Colonel Vize." The man in front of them, in a space suit, looked like he was military. He spoke in a gravelly voice.

"Who are you people?" demanded Deedee.

"We are the good guys." Colonel Vize smiled curtly.

"US intelligence?" Arno asked.

"All you need to know is, we are the good guys."

"Are you going to whack us?" Arno asked, looking from Vize to Gomez.

"We don't whack people. We're the good guys." Vize smiled again to reassure them.

"Then what are you going to do with us?" Deedee asked.

"Don't worry. You are safer with us than with the foreign agents you encountered down there."

"What are you going to do with the poles?" Arno asked.

"Sorry, that's classified information."

"Do you even know what you have there?" Arno pointed to the two containers that were stowed behind a net near the ceiling.

"What do you think we have there?" Colonel Vize asked, pointing with his thumb at the containers.

Arno and Deedee exchanged a quick glance. They were sure the colonel knew what he had in his possession.

"Unipolar elements," answered Arno.

"When did you figure that out?" Colonel Vize asked.

"Down in the mine," said Arno.

"How do you feel after your experience in the Time Hole?"

"You know about the Time Hole?" said Arno.

"Yes. How do you feel?"

"We're fine," said Deedee. "Other than suffering from occasional time vertigo."

"That's good."

"What are you going to do with the poles?" Deedee asked.

"That's classified."

"Bullshit!" erupted Deedee. "Are you going to make weapons from them or will you use them for peaceful endeavors?"

"What do you think the Chinese, Indians, or Brazilians would have done with them?"

Deedee and Arno looked at each other again. That was a question that had no good answer.

"And to put you at ease that we are the good guys, there was a Russian team waiting to ambush the

Chinese-Indian-Brazilian operatives and steal the poles from them. Embarrassingly, the Russians knew more than we knew about the poles. That's how we learned about the Time Hole."

"The Russians knew about the Time Hole and what it can do?" Arno asked worriedly.

"That's right," said Colonel Vize in his gravelly voice, sensing their quandary. "What we have here is out of this world, alien technology, and somehow you experienced it and survived."

The two specialists they had met down in the mine carrying the red cylindrical device climbed into the craft and sat in the pilot seats. They began energizing different systems, preparing for takeoff.

"I suggest you strap yourself in and connect your SLSs to the craft's supply," said Colonel Vize, as he connected his SLS to the craft ports on the side of his seat's armrest.

Deedee and Arno didn't know what would happen next. Chances were that they were leaving the Moon and were to be kept somewhere where they could not divulge what they knew. They connected themselves to the craft's supply of air and power, strapped themselves in, and made peace with their new reality.

The craft lifted and glided above the lunar surface in an obvious attempt to avoid detection. S18 was disappearing behind the horizon when they saw a small flash of light. Rings of seismic tremors radiated out on the lunar surface from where S18 had once been.

Deedee's eyes went wide and she elbowed Arno. He nodded as he saw the explosion as well. Hopefully, only the five already dead were buried in the underground nuclear explosion.

The craft gained some altitude but not much. At a certain point, it descended to a couple of meters above the ground, and Arno noticed that they were flying over the road leading to RABi. It was apparent that they were smoothing the road of any wheel tracks. On the Moon the dust raised by the rocket engines doesn't linger and it settled quickly down.

"Getting rid of the evidence that we once rode there," Arno said to Deedee.

She had a better view behind the craft. The road had become a smooth path.

"You are correct," said Colonel Vize. "The less anyone knows of your whereabouts and disappearance, the better you'll be. Trust me." He winked at them.

Trust him? That's not what they were feeling. Deedee and Arno looked at each other worriedly. Would they be the next ones to be erased?

Chapter 35.

Deedee opened her eyes and stared at the white ceiling, wondering where she was. She turned her head and recognized a recovery room in an infirmary somewhere. A monitor displayed digital green and red readings, most likely her health bio-signs. She turned her head and saw Arno in the other bed. Where were they? She couldn't lift her head. She felt groggy.

A nurse in light-blue hospital wear bent over her. "How do you feel, Deedee?"

The nurse looked familiar. "Where are we?" Deedee asked.

"In the infirmary at RABi."

Any other response would have been acceptable, but RABi? She sat up, feeling dizzy from the blood rush. "We're at RABi? How could we be at RABi?"

"Luckily, we found you in time, before you ran out of air."

Arno woke up in the next bed. "What...where are we?" Arno looked at Deedee and the nurse.

"We're at RABi, Arno. Can you believe this?" said Deedee, holding her head in her hands.

Arno rubbed his face with one hand. "We're alive. I would prefer to convalesce on Oahu, but RABi will have to do."

"What happened to us?" Deedee asked the nurse.

"We found you in the truck. Yesterday. You were unconscious."

"Where was the truck?" Arno asked.

"In garage #4."

"How did we get there?" Arno asked.

"According to Martha, you drove in yesterday but never came out of the cab. You can see the video later. Martha sounded the alarm and we brought you in. Other than having been unconscious, you're healthy."

"How long had we been missing?" Arno asked.

"About five days."

"What, we were missing for five days?" Deedee almost jumped from her bed.

"Yes, you're lucky to return and be alive. Where have you been?" the nurse asked.

Deedee opened her mouth to answer, but Arno spoke before she could say a word. "I wish we knew. I don't seem to remember anything." Arno looked at Deedee, shaking his head. "Do you remember anything, Deedee?"

She got the hint and said, "Where the hell have we been? I don't know, I can't remember." She buried her face in her hands.

"Is manager Lai around?" Arno asked.

The nurse turned pale and sad. "I'm afraid there has been an accident at S18, and manager Lai, Samir, and Randy, with three others from K204, are dead."

"What happened?"

"S18 blew up. One of the miners must have hit something with a drill and it detonated a nuke."

"A nuke? Whose nuke?" Arno asked.

"Nobody knows." The nurse shrugged. "It was deep underground, and the damage was localized to S18. K204 survived but badly shaken."

"You say Samir was there, too? What were they doing at S18, in a mine?" Deedee wanted to hear the official explanation.

"They were conducting an inspection."

Deedee and Arno exchanged knowing glances.

"Who were the other three, besides our people?" Deedee asked.

"Superintended Davi Vieyra, and two specialists, Gomez and Todug."

Deedee glanced at Arno again. They declared Gomez, if that was his real name, dead as well. A clean job.

"Who's in charge of the station?" Arno asked.

"Hector Garcia and Lola Sing are the acting managers."

"Do they want to talk to us?" Arno asked.

"No one said anything like that."

Deedee and Arno exchanged some more glances. Why should the acting managers get involved with their disappearance? The Earth team would take care of that.

"Is there an investigation or something?" Arno asked.

"Yes, there will be several teams coming from Earth to assess what happened and how to prevent this from happening again. They are due to arrive in two days."

"That's good," Arno said. "Then we can get out of here."

"Yes, you're clear." The nurse looked one more time at the monitors and smiled at them.

Deedee and Arno, dressed in their generalist red jumpsuits, were alone in the break room having coffee. Arno leaned back and stared at the flat panels on the ceiling showing a blue sky with puffy white clouds passing by.

"We finally managed to sleep together," said Arno.

"When did we do that? Deedee asked, amused.

"In the infirmary," Arno replied.

"How could I forget?" Deedee patted Arno's hand. "There is a special spacecraft coming here in two days. The brass needs answers for what happened here."

"As expected," Arno said. "Do you still remember what happened?"

"Sure, but something is bugging me."

"Something is bugging me, too." Arno took Deedee by the hand and motioned her to walk out of there.

Arno took the corridor heading for SR G. Deedee looked at him with raised eyebrows.

"How about a stroll outside?" he asked her, and he placed a finger over his lips. She nodded in acknowledgement.

They were suited and standing in front of the airlock to exit to the outside.

"Martha, this is Arno," he said into his mic.

"Roger, Arno. What's up? On the monitor I can see you kids suited for an outside walk. I'd think you would have had enough of the outdoors."

"We feel claustrophobic in here and would like to see larger spaces," said Arno.

"Go ahead, and don't get lost again."

"I promise."

Chapter 36.

A minute later they stepped outside onto the fine sand of the Moon. It was still night, but the sky sparkled with stars.

"Let's take a rover and drive around," Arno said, pointing to several golf-cart rovers parked under a shed. After they sat down in one of them, he drove it toward the greenhouses.

The greenhouses were dormant during the lunar night, with the exception of the few of them that grew mushrooms. In those greenhouses, the atmosphere was breathable and maintained at a balmy 20^0C. They entered through an airlock into one of the mushroom farms. It was dark inside, but there was enough light coming from the Milky Way to penetrate the thick plastic membrane of the greenhouse. Arno and Deedee unsealed and opened their helmets. It smelled like mushrooms and artificial manure, but the air was breathable.

"Is this your idea of romance, Arno? Take me to a dark place that smells like fungi and dung?"

"What do you expect from a fun-guy like me?" said Arno. "But it is under the stars." He turned off the power on his suit.

Deedee turned off her power, while chuckling. "Do you think they'll buy it?"

"Unless we find a broom closet without cameras and mics, this will have to do."

"What's on your mind?"

"You know that we're observed around the clock."

"I figured as much," said Deedee.

"When the Earth investigation team arrives, they'll question us intensively. Perhaps we'll have to take a polygraph test."

"No doubt."

"The problem is, what do we say about the S18 accident?" Arno asked.

"The truth?" Deedee volunteered.

"You mean to tell them that we fell into a Time Hole that no one even knew existed, that we were invisible to everyone else, that we stole a craft and went to S18, that we witnessed five deaths—three of whom were secret agents—and that we were taken by other secret agents in their craft. They took the unipolar elements from us, nuked S18, and then they released us, unharmed. After being missing for five days."

Deedee stared at him for a while before she said, "Kind of unbelievable, isn't it?"

"Unbelievable would be good, if there were not five deaths and one nuclear explosion involved. Six, if you count Gomez." The corners of Arno's mouth bent down.

"So you think we should leave out the part about us taking the craft to S18 and everything we witnessed there?"

Arno nodded. "Samir was the only one who saw us while in the altered state of time, and he told Lai. They're dead, and nobody else knows about our appearance-disappearance."

"I think Colonel Vize knows," Deedee said. "And maybe Gomez."

"How do you know?" Arno asked.

"Vize mentioned the Time Hole. And Gomez saw it, too, down below in the mine when we got out of it. Who knows, maybe Gomez even video-recorded us. I bet Vize and his agents here have scrubbed all the evidence that we appeared or took the craft."

"And are giving the impression that we're just two lunatics," said Arno thoughtfully.

"Yeah. It was either that or whack us. But they are the good guys," said Deedee with a conspiratorial smile. "They only gave us narcotics or something."

"In that case, no one around here really knows what happened," said Arno. "Except for some other secret agents here at RABi." Arno thought for a moment. "The five bodies were vaporized by the nuke. I doubt they'll find anything underground."

"There is one more person who is not dead, who heard about our appearance," said Deedee.

"Martha?"

"Uh-huh," Deedee said. "Lai asked her about us being around, but I bet she will not talk about it. She's one of the good guys' agents."

"Then that simplifies everything. We were driving merrily to K204 and then at some point, we don't remember anything anymore. Maybe a gas leaked into our suits, intoxicated us, caused illusions and amnesia, and somehow we managed to come back to RABi. We wished we knew more about our whereabouts." He shook his head in sorrow.

"Being gone for five days will raise some eyebrows," said Deedee. "I wonder what the good guys did to us from the last time we could remember, when they were sweeping the road back to RABi?"

"Probably they drugged us and questioned us about our experiences in the Time Hole," said Arno. "The likely did some analysis, after which they figured we didn't present any danger and let us go. And now we need to come up with a story that will not invite many more questions."

"Are you sure you're not one of those secret agents?"

"No, I just want to save my skin." Arno smiled. "How about you? Are you one of them?"

Deedee shook her head. "Aside from some other probing questions, which we may not know how to answer because we don't remember, the story is good enough."

"No one saw us going to S18 or anywhere, for that matter." Arno nodded, satisfied at what they'd tell the investigators.

"I agree," said Deedee. "Except they saw CRAB-A fly away with the fuel we used to carry on the truck."

"CRAB-A is a mystery," said Arno. "It flew away piloted by who knows who, and probably along with CRAB-B were destroyed in the explosion. Also, what are the chances that the records show the volume in the trailer's tanks when we left to be the same as the tanks are now?"

"How about the codes we entered to get in and out of the craft?"

"Wiped off. I'm sure."

Deedee nodded. "How did we get back in the truck and back to the garage? We left the truck in hangar A."

"Probably we did," said Arno. "When we re-entered the truck it reversed to normal time, became visible, and we rode it back into the garage. Like sleepwalkers."

"If no one says anything different, that's a good explanation not to be mentioned," said Deedee. "Now let's talk about what the hell really happened."

Chapter 37.

"What do you mean, what really happened?" Arno asked.

"The poles and the Time Hole," said Deedee.

"The unipolar elements are in someone's possession. Who knows whose? They didn't kill us, so they must be the good guys, and that's good."

"Do you think they will be used for weaponry?" Deedee wondered.

"Like invisible armies and stuff?" Arno screwed his face as if to say anything is possible.

"What are these unipolar elements?"

"I don't think they are alien-built. They are natural elements."

"How did they get on the Moon?"

"Crashed into it," said Arno. "However, I think they were used by aliens for space travel on an asteroid serving as a space craft. The poles are what's left of it."

"If that's the truth, how did they use them for space travel?"

"Here is my theory," said Arno. "Space travel is difficult because of the vast distances between stars. More speed doesn't do any good. Even if we invent rockets that can go faster and faster, when a craft reaches about ten percent of the speed of light, even a pebble colliding with the craft would be catastrophic. The amount of kinetic energy would blow the ship into pieces. Therefore, instead of working on more powerful rockets for more speed, why not delay time instead?"

"What? How?"

"The two poles create a Time Hole in between them. Imagine a craft that has the two poles on board. It separates the poles, and a Time Hole is created in the middle of the craft. The farther apart the poles are, the bigger the Time Hole to accommodate the astronauts and all the essential hardware. Outside the Hole, that craft remains the same, unless the Hole swallows the whole craft, and then only the poles are left to see. The ship and its time-arrested entities travel as fast as they can practically go. Inside the Hole, the astronauts live in their own time dimension. They could slow time or they could stop time completely."

"Wow, do you realize what you're saying? If the craft lasts that long, they could travel for a thousand years, ten thousand years, and when they get to the destination, it will be as if they had left their home planet seconds earlier."

"Exactly." Arno's eyes brightened at the thought. "And since you mentioned that the craft has to last for thousands of years, what could be better than an asteroid to serve as the ship? Maybe that's why there wasn't any craft to be discovered where the poles were found."

"Just more rocks and dust," said Deedee.

Arno nodded.

"However, there is a problem with your theory," said Deedee. "What civilization can wait for thousands of years to hear from the mission? By then, the civilization may be extinct. Only the astronauts' scientific curiosity would be satisfied. Of course, on the other hand, it would be good for colonizing other planets."

"True, but you forgot one important aspect of the Time Hole," said Arno. "It's like having your cake and eating it, too. You can use the Time Hole to stop time on the spacecraft. The mission is launched today, and it returns home after the time it takes to explore the new planet, say a month, although it traveled thousands of years in space. The astronauts and the parent planet are of the same age as when they left. In reality, the explorers visit another star system in real time, as it would be on their home planet."

"Oh, God! Do you think that's possible? Can you imagine the possibility of space exploration?"

"Theoretically, yes," said Arno, proud of his explanation.

"God! Theorists envision wormholes to go through the far reaches of the universe, and all it takes is manipulating time." Deedee exhaled and shook her head. "We're so primitive, compared to the aliens who invented this technology."

"Well, I don't think they started in their civilization all that intelligent, just like us," said Arno philosophically. "Question is, where did they find those poles?"

"If they are natural elements, then we have only two of them. Hardly enough for colonizing the universe."

"That's true, but two is better than none."

"What you just told me—is it fantasy or do you know it for a fact?" Deedee asked.

Arno gave a little chuckle. "It is an educated deduction. Remember when I was in the Time Hole and I saw myself as an old man?"

"That gave me hope that we'd survive our—"Deedee stopped abruptly. "Don't tell me you know this from your old self?"

Arno nodded. "Not all I'd know at that age. I spent a brief time with my old self, mostly gasping at my wrinkles, and I didn't have time to explore all his— my—future knowledge. Come to think of it, I was on another planet, far away from Earth at the time. I was so shocked at what I was experiencing that I didn't take in all that was around me."

"Can you recall any more details about the technology you were using to travel to another planet?"

Arno shook his head. "I wish I did, but I only had a glimpse into the future. Details were not included."

"Talking about time stopping or slowing down," said Deedee. "Do you remember the Gold Rush incident 10 years ago?"

"Uh-huh," said Arno. "The disappearance of the seven astronauts from the Gold Rush base on the near side of the Moon. What about it?"

"There were rumors that Gold Rush experienced a five-second time delay between the clocks on board and those of the Bruno space station orbiting around the Moon and Houston Mission Control."

"Yes, but that was never verified," Arno said.

"Of course not," said Deedee. "They can't even explain where the seven astronauts are. Gold Rush was deserted when the rescue team arrived. And Gold Rush and the crater is in is now off-limits. Do you think that's what happened to them? They fell into a Time Hole?"

"If they did, they weren't as lucky as we are," said Arno. "There are a lot of mysteries to be discovered here on the Moon. Let's count our blessings that we came out of this alive."

Deedee stepped closer to him and grabbed him by the front of his vest. "You know, you're not only tall and good-looking, but you're smart, too."

"What a shock, huh?" said Arno, pretending to be humble.

Deedee pulled herself up and kissed him on the lips. "You know, these scientific explanations are kind of exciting and exhausting." She looked into his eyes. "What do you say we go back and sleep together again?"

"Sure, but this time not in the infirmary."

The End

Bonus: **Free eBook**.

Thank you for reading my book. As a token of my appreciation you may choose any of my e-books listed below and get it for Free on your Kindle. All you need to do is e-mail me at mit.sandru@yahoo.com , stating, which book you wish to receive for Free. What's the catch? No catch, but your honest review will be appreciated. Your e-mail will not be sold or used for spam. Occasionally, I'll send you e-mails announcing a new book release or a good deal for my books and that's all.

If you enjoyed this book and would like to help other readers with your comments please write a review on Amazon, which I appreciate very much. Amazon books link.

For more information about my books and my art please visit my website: sandru.com

Other Books by Sandru (Mit, DG, or Dumitru)

Science Fiction

Gold Rush Mystery (Terraspantion Chronicles, Bk. 1) by Mit Sandru.

America is back on the Moon, and we intend to stay and establish a self-sustaining permanent base for tourism and mining. The work is challenging, the environment is deadly, but the astronauts Mia, Geo and Roby succeed in building the moon base, even if they landed in a mysterious crater.

Time Hole, (Terraspantion Chronicles, Bk. 2) by Mit Sandru.

Mining on the moon is a hazardous affair. Deedee and Arno, two lunar generalists, find perils beyond what they signed up for when they travel on the lunar surface at night . . . on the dark side of the Moon. Time will not be the same after they fall into the *Time Hole*.

Sferogyls (Timurud Book 1) by Mit Sandru

The Maggotroll Empire invades the Sferogyls' planet. The Sferogyls are unarmed and have no defense against the imperial battleships. The gods resurrect Timurud and send him to help the peaceful Sferogyls fight the invaders. Will the Sferogyls win the war in space and defend their planet, or perish?

Folding Reality, by Mit Sandru. Time Travel Adventure

Mike the insurance salesman experiences perilous time travel experiences just by folding a piece of paper. He is crucified on Golgotha, almost gassed at Auschwitz, marooned in a Russian capsule going to the Moon.

Teen, Children Fantasy and Sci-Fi

Arboregal, the Lorn Tree, by D.G. Sandru.

Four youngsters, Melissa, Perry, Nathan and Michelle materialize in a desolate world where giant, mile-high trees, support all life. They find shelter in the Lorn Tree among the Lorns. Soon after they discover that an evil spirit, Hellferata, wants them dead. Fearful Lorns want to expel the youngsters from their tree, which would be a dead sentence since monsters roam the land at night.

Will their ingenuity, cunning, and courage help them escape, or will Hellferata mete out her wrath before they can escape?

Paranormal, Mystery, Thriller

The Pregnant Pope (Book 1 TIO Series), by Mit Sandru.

The 92-year-old Pope is pregnant. He hasn't undergone any medical procedures, but he carries a fetus in his abdomen. Is this a case of self-cloning, or a mutation? Is this an Immaculate Conception, or Satan's work? Find out how Claire, Travis, and Prescott solve this mystery and the bizarre outcome.

The Devolution of Adam and Eve (Book 2 TIO Series) by Mit Sandru

A pandemic causes billions of people to lose their minds. The world's government health agencies cannot identify the pathogen and develop an antidote. It comes from another realm, and only Claire, Prescott, and Travis can solve this enigma. Will they prevent the end of humanity before it's too late?

The Vlad V, Blue Blood Vampires Thriller & Romance

Vampire (Vlad V, Bk 1) by Mit Sandru.

Meeting a vampire isn't something that happens every night, even on the New York City subway. But never in her wildest dreams did Cat Sanders ever expect to meet the vampire Vlad V Draculesti and survive the encounter. Instead, she became his confidant. Why was she so lucky?

R.I.P., The Death of a Vampire (Vlad V, Bk 2) by Mit Sandru.

Vlad V Draculesti is dying because of an incident that happened decades ago. Unfortunately for Vlad V, the US intelligence agencies investigate him to find out his true identity, and centuries old life. Will Cat Sanders and vampire friends be able to help him die in peace, or will Vlad be discovered for being a vampire and die in a US Federal research laboratory?

Vampire Slayers (Vlad V, Bk 3) by Mit Sandru.

Cat Sanders is a billionaire, but not all is well. Her nemesis, Veronica Seyler, allied with a vampire-slayer drug cult, demands extortion money or she will be killed.

Cat's vampire friend, Angelique, comes to her aid. But the cult is more cunning and dangerous than even her vampire friend could handle. Would Cat and Angelique be able to come out of this alive even if Cat pays the ransom?

Vampires of Transylvania (Vlad V, Bk 4) by Mit Sandru

Cat Sanders has a simple task: spread Vlad V's ashes in Transylvania at midnight, during full moon. But in Transylvania Vlad V has centuries old enemies who take her and her friend Tudor hostage, placing them in iron cages among zombies and proto-vampires. Will they be able to escape from the blood sucking proto-vampires and flesh-eating zombies, or become zombies themselves?

The Queen of Vampires: A New Queen Arises (Vlad V, Bk 5) by Mit Sandru

The Vampire Queen, Eleonore von Schwarzenberg, is bloodthirsty and vengeful on Cat Sanders and her friends. She plans the most painful death for them. Cat and her friends find themselves entrapped and helpless to avoid her wrath.

Will Cat and her friends be able to escape and survive the Queen of Vampires' fury?

Non-Fiction, Biography, Political

Escape from Communism, by Dumitru Sandru, a True Story and Commentary.

Life under communism is cruel and inhumane. Commit the smallest political infraction, and the secret police will arrest you. The only ray of hope is the West, but it is a crime to escape by crossing the border illegally, and anyone caught is beaten and imprisoned, sometimes even shot. This is my story of what happened and how I reached freedom.

Coloring Book

Abstract Dreams: Coloring Book 1 (Sandru's Art) by Dumitru Sandru

Reward your soul with the smooth and pleasing lines of Abstract Dreams

T-Shirts and other stuff:

Sandru's Shop or Sandru's Products

Visit my e-Gallery at:
http://dumitru-sandru.artistwebsites.com/
http://www.artistrising.com/galleries/Sandru

About Dumitru "Mit" Sandru

He was born in the greater area of Transylvania in the last century. He is an artist, composer, and author. He paints in the classical, surreal, and modern styles, and most of the music Dumitru composes is of the New Age flavor. As an author, he prefers to write Science-Fiction, Paranormal, and Teen/Children Fantasy novels.

Dumitru resides in California with his wife. They have one daughter and two grandsons.

Visit him at **sandru.com**